YOU'RE THE ONE I
DON'T WANT

CARRIE AARONS

Do you want your **FREE** Carrie Aarons eBook?

All you have to do is **<u>sign up for my newsletter</u>**, and you'll immediately receive your free book!

For CMK.
This has been the hardest, most rewarding, most incredible time in my
life, and it's all because of you.

1

ANNABELLE

"This carpet looks like baby poop. It is awful."

I sniff haughtily at the air, trying to make sure that said carpet doesn't also smell like baby poop. I have no idea why someone would choose this color to don the floor of their bedroom, and I've never been one to placate people for the simple courtesy of kindness.

"Anna!" Ramona smiles through her teeth while fear of pissing off the clients widens her eyes. "What she means is that this color doesn't exactly complement your color palette. I think we could go with more of a mauve or a gray, and it would bring out the tone of the room much better."

Sure, that was the nice way of putting it. But no one would ever use the word nice to describe me. After hand-holding and reassuring the homeowners for another five minutes, while I stand there taking notes on her design ideas, Ramona pulls me aside by the audio equipment.

"Anna, honey, you know I love your eye. And your honesty. But ... we run a family TV show here. You have to tone down the cynicism a bit." Her eye twinkle as she winks at me.

I shrug. "You love me because I say the things you can't. People love my dry honesty. And plus, this carpet really does look like baby poop."

Ramona, her blond hair waving around her shoulders, hoots out a laugh. "Where did you learn such confidence? I wish I was half as sure about myself when I was your age. And ... you're right. This is an awful carpet. Which is why it will be so fun to redesign this house."

My boss, a woman on her way to forty who dresses like a hippie and completely pulls it off, pats me on the shoulder and walks over to her husband, the other star of the show. Their foreheads press together as she looks over the tile samples he's picked, and my heart surges with jealousy and admiration.

Sometimes, I still can't believe I work so closely with the two biggest stars of the Flipping Channel. An entire channel dedicated to interior design and rehabbing homes, Ramona and James Hart have been the darlings from the start, with their wildly popular show *Hart & Home*. I'd applied to be a production assistant on the show in my freshman year at Austin and had been hired. From there, I'd done everything possible to get in front of Ramona and James, to make them see how much better my design eye was than the people they were paying to consult on projects.

My big break had come on a rustic farmhouse, not unlike the one my grandparents had owned when I was a child. James couldn't figure out how to preserve the hundred-year-old wood that had been used to construct the outside of the house. After researching, and talking to both my father and Harper's grandma, who was technically my step-grandmother now, I'd given him the tip of hand-scraping the old layer of paint off, and then re-painting and staining it.

He'd listened, and then made me help the crew who hand-scraped the paint off. It took days, carefully stripping that wood, but it had finally made them take notice of me.

And now, I'm their right-hand girl. I'm on every weekly episode, and I'm kind of living in my own fifteen minutes of fame. I even have a blue check mark next to my name on Twitter and Instagram.

But Ramona is wrong about one thing. I'm not confident, and I sure as hell have no idea who I am. Ever heard of the phrase, "fake it till you make it?" That is me in a nutshell. I've been that way since my mother left us when I was ten years old, stomping through life like an in-the-flesh Regina George, demanding to have her way with the world.

I'm a bitch on the outside so that no one can see the mess I am on the inside. It's not a new story, it's not even a particularly interesting one. But it does earn me both hilarious memes and vitriol on social media, so I guess I am kind of getting what I want.

I'd hitched my wagon to Ramona and James' in the hopes that one day, I would be the most successful and respected interior designer in the country, and maybe even the world. So far, as a second-semester college junior, I was more than on track. Most days, I looked in the mirror and repeated my goals and dreams to myself. Because really, they were all I had. My spite and drive were the things that fueled me.

Everyone who had ever counted me out, or left me hanging, would see how great I could become.

"Hey, Anna, come over here and tell me what you think of these, huh?" James motions me over.

The male part of my boss team was thick and broad, a former linebacker in college, he was prematurely graying. But, like all men, age only made him look dapper. His once-muscled figure still kind of dipped and curved in the right way, and his hair color added some wisdom.

He held backsplash tiles for the kitchen since we were going to rip out the horrible peach-colored rose design that donned this couple's breakfast nook. One was gray, another a traditional white subway pattern, and the last was a navy paisley that seemed a little high-class for the homeowners.

But in the end, I point to the navy. Everyone should feel upscale in their own home, even if someone had to pick classy options for them.

James' phone buzzes as Ramona takes a sip of her coffee. "Gah, this is cold. Can I get a new cup, please?"

A production assistant rushes forward to take her travel mug, and I smirk. That used to be me, not so long ago. Look how far I've risen in such a short time. Take that, naysayers.

"No crap! This is awesome." James is still looking at his phone.

"What's that, babe?" Ramona rubs her husband's back. Even after four kids and countless years together, they're still so in love it makes me want to gag at times.

"Our ball team drafted the rights to an awesome outfielder with a swing that could rival Babe Ruth's! Shit, we're going to be so good in a couple of seasons."

The mention of baseball sets my teeth on edge. I may have been a cheerleader in high school, but sports were not my thing. Especially since most of the guys who played any one of them were complete jackasses.

"What's his name, baby? Maybe we can congratulate him on the feed. We love to support Texas!" Ramona already had her phone out, ready to tweet to her four million followers.

James reads his phone again. "Uh ... the kid's name is ... oh here it is, Boone Graham."

My stomach drops out. Completely plummets to my feet. That name rolling off of his lips blindsides me so hard, it's like I've been hit upside the head by a freight train.

I wobble to the right, using the side of the production van to steady myself. My throat is dry, and even though it's only fifty-six degrees, my entire body starts to sweat.

I broke Boone Graham's heart, once upon a time. We haven't spoken since I betrayed him. And now, he was coming home.

2

BOONE

For some reason, I never thought I'd ever go back to Texas.

I know it was a stupid thought for me to even harbor, because the place is in the continental United States, and eventually, I would have probably passed through or had to come home for a visit. But I truly put this place out of my head when I left all those years ago.

The humidity blasts me in the face as I walk out of the automatic airport doors, and even though it's probably in the fifties and it's only January, this is a far cry from the below ball-freezing temps of Pennsylvania.

When I'd gotten accepted to Penn State my senior year of high school, I'd counted down the days until I could get out of Haven. That place had built me, and then one singular action by a nightmare of a woman crushed me. Scratch that, she was a girl. No one that spiteful and immature could ever be called a woman.

But I'd always thought I would stay on the East Coast. My future was bright, I was talented enough and had the work ethic to make it to the majors. That much had been clear since the time I was about twelve and my hitting clicked into place.

I thought that Pennsylvania had been the place for me. And it had been. I liked the cold temperatures, the no-nonsense attitudes of the people who lived there. I liked the quick wit and sharp tongues of East Coasters, and that no one let you too close and you could feel free to do the same. I'd gone in as a true freshman, won a championship my first year out. I'd planned to get drafted there, play for one of the big cities.

And then I'd gone in the first round of the draft. To a farm team just one level under the biggest franchise in Texas.

Texas was in your business from the start. Everyone wanted to know your business and your mama's business. Texas had a smile on its face and a knife behind its back. They might serve you a warm peach cobbler and sweet tea, but don't be surprised if there was poison in both. Texas was slow and sensual, far too sneaky for my liking.

I pull at the collar of my button-down and suit jacket, annoyed that my agent insisted I wear a three-piece on the flight. But as I near the chauffeur with a sign that reads Boone Graham in typed letters, I send my agent a silent, begrudged thank you. Because there are about a dozen reporters standing next to the car I'm about to make a dive for, all asking questions at the top of their lungs.

"Boone, welcome to Austin. What do you think of the franchise you've been drafted into?"

"Boone, I'm with Her Austin Life. Tell our readers, do you have a girlfriend?"

"What are your feelings on being drafted first, over skill players like Johnston and Hydro?"

"Do you think you'll measure up in the majors?"

Words bombard my ears, and all I want to do is cover them

and duck my head under the in-flight neck pillow now attached to my luggage, but they'd for sure write about that so I refrain.

I like the franchise and am honored that they drafted me with their top pick.

I don't have a girlfriend, thank God.

Being drafted first leaves a lot of expectations, which I hope I can measure up to.

And speaking of measuring up, it's the one thing I've been worried about the most. Can I compete with this caliber of players?

But I don't say any of this. Instead, I get into the car, giving the driver a quick nod of thanks as he takes my bags and makes quick work of getting us out of this clown show.

The feeling sinks in, those anxious goose bumps I've been getting ever since my name was announced on national television. I've dreamt of this day, have dug my heels in and done the work. I know that the hard work is only just beginning, both on and off the field, but a part of me feels fulfilled for having made it this far.

And yet ... I'd thrown out the one condition I had to my new team and the owners who had such faith in me. I needed to hold a degree in my hand before I'd step out onto the field and play ball for them. Because of my baseball schedule and the wrench getting drafted had thrown into my education, I was in my fifth year of school. But thankfully, I am going to graduate at the end of it. Most anyone who heard that clause in my contract would think I was absolutely insane. There were athletes striving, killing themselves daily to sign a pro contract and make millions.

But what happened if that didn't pan out? If they made it to the highest level and flopped? Where would that leave them?

No one knew why it was so important for me to finish

college, and I'd like to leave it that way. I only had one semester left, and then baseball could have me for good.

The black sedan zips us through downtown Austin and out onto the highway, and the road cuts through and right on top of pastures and rolling fields. This is the part of Texas I missed. Sitting on my parent's back porch, listening to the crickets and my dad play guitar on the rare nights that he was sober enough to do so.

The driver maneuvers us past exit after exit, and I know we're headed to the Texas baseball institution where I'll someday play, and I should be alert, but after the long flight, I kind of want to take a nap.

And then her face is in front of my own two eyes, and I have to blink in surprise. The back of my head hits the headrest, I'm so shaken up. I just didn't expect to see her right there, and yet, how could I forget?

Annabelle Mills, the nightmare of a girl I told you about.

She is on the outskirts of a billboard rising high over the highway, one that features that famous couple who flipped old farmhouses. The main focal point of the huge obnoxious advertisement was supposed to be Ramona and James Hart, but anyone could see that Annabelle was the real star.

A brunette bombshell with the sparkle of a Texas beauty queen, my ex ... well, whatever we'd been, was someone you could never quite take your eye off of. When she walked into the room, jaws dropped. While you were talking to her, you were always semi-conscious of the fact that she might be the most breathtaking sight you've ever seen.

But under all of that gloss and gorgeousness, there was a cold, nasty heart.

How could I have forgotten that we were about to live in the same city?

No, don't lie, dammit. I hadn't forgotten. I'd simply hoped I could avoid her forever, just like I had since the day I'd dumped her on the front steps of the high school.

Annabelle Mills had broken my heart, and it hasn't been quite the same since.

The thing was, I didn't plan on loving again, after the torture she'd put me through.

So who cared if the thing was fractured and unused?

"I'm sorry, do you live here now? Because I thought I was living with my nomadic girlfriend, not her stepsister."

Cain walks out of his bedroom in a towel, and I roll my eyes at his back as he goes to the fridge, rummaging around for a snack.

"Keep your panties on, Kent. I'm waiting for said nomad to get home, and she gave me a key for when I had to escape my awful, slutty roommate."

Was it strange that he and I had slept together before we'd even known that Harper had existed, and now she was his girlfriend and my stepsister? Maybe. But the three of us didn't let it affect our relationships. I was still friends with Cain, as we had been since childhood, and Harper and I were closer than ever.

Who would have thought? I'd hated Harper on principle when she'd moved to Haven. Then I'd hated her, even more, when my dad started dating her mom. But, over time, both she and her mom had grown on me, and now ... they were the family I'd lost when my parents had split up. And also the family I'd never had but wished for.

"What if I wanted to see my girlfriend when she got back? Ever think of that? I haven't seen her since she took off for San Diego two weeks ago."

I flick him off, my middle finger standing proud. "I need her more right now. You can get your rocks off later. Sisters before misters, remember?"

He grumbles as he takes a bite out of an apple. "Yeah, whatever. So, slutty roommate is still going at it?"

I set my phone down, which I've been monitoring for texts from Harper with any update on when she'll be home. "God, it's like the girl's vagina doesn't know when to quit. I swear, the other day, there were three different guys in and out of our room. One of them she did in the shower, but still! And the creep asked to borrow my towel! Gross!"

Cain laughs and walks back to his room, presumably to put on clothes. He lives in a one-bedroom apartment in the on-campus housing units and is usually shacked up with Harper when she isn't off on a writing adventure. I know they're both anxious about what's to come. Cain just won the college football championship as a second-year starter, since he red-shirted our freshman year, and his popularity, which was already on the rise, has blown up. He's going to enter the draft next year to go pro, and Harper has already told me how nervous this makes her. She already has to share him with Texas and the college scene, but when he's making millions, she'll have to share him with the world.

"I like sex as much as the next person, but it sounds like this girl might be a nymphomaniac. Literally. Three partners in one day, that's a lot even for me." Cain comes back out attired in Austin football sweats from head to toe.

"Says the guy who once made a sex bet." I roll my eyes, yet again.

Rolling my eyes is one of my signature moves.

His eyes go sharp. "Hey, that is all behind me."

Before I can tell that I know and that I also know that he loves my stepsister, said stepsister walks through the door.

Or should I say, stumbles through the door carrying a suitcase way too big for her pixie frame. "Uh, hello, is anyone going to help me?"

Harper's annoyed voice is cut off. Not by her boyfriend helping her, but rather sweeping her off of her feet and planting a huge kiss on her lips.

"Cain!" She giggles and hits him as if she's embarrassed.

I would be more grossed out if I wasn't so green with envy. "All right, can you not? Third wheel in the room here."

Cain sets her down, gives me a stink eye, and walks toward their bedroom. Before he enters it, he looks back over his shoulder. "I'll be waiting in our bed. And just know, I have missed you *a lot* over the past two weeks."

"Hi." Harper puts her hand on my arm as she passes to get a drink of water.

Because of how we both grew up, separately of course, we aren't the most touchy-feely people. But we have come to rely on each other like sisters, or I hope we have. At least, that's how I feel. My relationship with Harper is the closest female bond I have in my life.

"Hey." I bite my lip. I want to get into why I've been here waiting for her, but I'm also not the most open book you've ever met.

"So ... you need to talk. Spill." And Harper has zero subtlety.

Which is probably why our friendship works.

I take a deep breath. "Boone is coming to Texas."

I can't believe his name has left my lips. It's not as if I still don't think about him weekly, but I haven't talked to anyone about him in such a long time. In fact, I don't know that I ever spoke to anyone about our breakup. If it qualifies as a breakup.

I mean, my heart was broken, so it definitely qualifies as something.

An unreadable emotion flicks over Harper's features. "Hm ... why?"

"Apparently, he got drafted by the major league team in Texas. They want him to play for the farm team in Austin."

She nods her head, and my heart skips a beat waiting for her to calm me down. "Well, Austin is a big town. So you probably won't even run into him. You can avoid him ... if you want to."

Do I want to? I guess it's what we both want to know. "I haven't seen him since he graduated. He hates me, Harp."

Her nose wrinkles. "You do know it's totally awkward for me to talk to you about this? Because ... you kind of cheated on him with my boyfriend. Who you slept with."

I'm glad we're so open, sometimes to a fault. I shrug. "I don't care if you don't. You're secure with Cain, so please don't make this weird. I need a therapist and you're the closest thing I've got."

Harper gives me a small smile. "Yeah, I guess I don't really care. I was just pointing it out. And I bet you he doesn't hate you. *But*, if you want to find out if he does, I think you have that opportunity now. You know where he'll be, you can find him if you want. The question is, is that what you want?"

She echoes my thoughts back to me. I honestly don't know. When I think about coming face-to-face with Boone Graham, it makes my knees shake and bile rise up the back of my throat. It makes my heart skip a beat and my stomach turn over like I've just begun the descent on the biggest roller coaster in the world.

I get up from their kitchen table and gather my bag. "All right, I'm getting out of here before Cain comes out here naked and drags you into that bedroom."

Harper laughs, but I'm almost positive I hear a moan as I walk out the door.

A fifteen-minute walk across campus gets me to my dorm, where, *thank God*, my roommate and her man friend have vacated the premises. I immediately unzip my thigh-high suede boots, slip the off-the-shoulder sweater over my head, and use a makeup wipe to clean my face. As much as I might look as made up as a beauty queen during the day, I am really most comfortable in my sweatpants with zit cream on.

Not that I'd ever let anyone, besides a select few, see my varnish and shine at anything less than one hundred percent.

I boot up my computer as I slide under the fluffy blush pink comforter on my dorm-issued extra-long twin bed, with every intention of reading about Boone's draft status and signing.

But ... I can't. I realize that I don't know if I want to hear about him yet. I realize that, even though how we ended was mostly my fault, I'm not sure if what he did to my heart can be forgiven either.

So I fall into old habits. I can't help it, it's my dirty little secret. My kryptonite.

I type in the URL for LinkedIn, and once I'm on the website, I type her name.

She has two new posts and a video, all of them having to do with some conference she's attending. Which of course she was asked to be the keynote speaker at.

My mother. Heather Nelson.

After she left my dad and me, she reverted back to her maiden name. As if she was never really a Mills at all. As if we never even really belonged to her. As if she never belonged to us.

The tightness in my chest aches, reverberating down my limbs and poisoning my blood, making me slam the computer shut. Per usual, I curse myself for visiting her page. At least I didn't go to her website, where everyone sings her praises like she is the messiah of information technology and cyber risk.

But I have to do it. I have to remind myself why I should never let someone so close again. I learned that lesson a long time ago.

If my own mother didn't want me, it was possible that no one did.

This loud, student-filled bar is literally the last place on earth I want to be.

Country music is piercing my eardrums, I've been stepped on by no less than three stiletto heels, the Pepsi I'm sipping is flat, and one of the guys on my new team is trying to compare himself to me in every statistical category that exists in baseball.

"Yeah, but you must've hit more home runs than that? I mean, they wouldn't have drafted you." This meathead keeps trying to fuck with me and I can feel my fists curling.

"Hey, Boone, let's hit the bar." Hudson Shem raises an eyebrow, trying to let me know he's rescuing me.

Hudson is the relief pitcher who has been around the Austin farm team for two years now waiting for a chance at The Show, better known as the major league of baseball. I've only been around a week, and most of that has been harassing the moving company for my stuff that is stuck on a truck somewhere ... but he and I have connected at the three practices I've participated in.

"Yeah, I could use a drink." I swing my big body out of the

booth it's been cramped in for an hour and breathe a sigh of relief.

As we walk to the bar, skirting around half-naked girls and drunk frat bros, I clap him on the shoulder. "Thanks, man. I needed that. Is he always that much of a dick?"

"Who, O'Donnell? Yeah, he's always that much of a dick. Just ignore him. He's got a weed problem and falls into slumps like it's his job. He'll never make it to The Show, take joy in that."

Hudson may be a relief pitcher, but he's built like a point guard. He's about six five, wiry but built, and has a mass of hair that hangs past his shoulders. I know what it's like to have eyes on you everywhere you go, whether it's because of my looks or my future profession, but the buzz of attraction around Hudson as he moves through the bar is next level.

He signals the bartender for a beer and turns to me. "You want a Heineken?"

I shake him off. "No, just a Pepsi."

"Staying sober tonight?"

More like every night, but I don't like to make that public. Actually, I don't like to make anything but my on the field work public. Because once you put something out there for people to know, they ask questions. And questions bring trouble.

"Something like that." I keep it simple.

We move to the side of the bar where it's actually a decibel quieter and I can hear myself think.

Hudson takes a sip of beer and clears his throat. "So, you all settled in?"

I chuckle. "Fuck no. The moving company lost my shit. I think I'm living in an apartment that used to be owned by a hoarder because I keep finding newspapers from nineteen eighty in every closet. Also, the university doesn't seem to understand that while I'm not a student-athlete, I'm still an athlete. Apparently, even though I play for a professional sports team,

I'm not eligible for a schedule that works with my practices. But hey, I'm here."

We both laugh at my misfortune. "So, why did you come out tonight?"

I shrug. "Figured it was probably a good idea to bond with the team a little bit. I always find that if you're at least friendly outside of the locker room, you play better together on the field."

Hudson nods. "I don't disagree. Can't believe you're going to finish college though. With your bat, you'd probably be called up in a few months. Hasn't anyone told you you're holding your career up by insisting on a degree?"

"Only every single time I talk to my agent. But it's something I have to do."

He looks at me like I'm crazy. Sadly, I'm used to this. No one will understand why I have to get a teaching degree before I'll let a team sign me to a million-dollar contract.

"Whatever, man. Do you. Meanwhile, I think I'm gonna do one of these girls tonight." Hudson checks out a blonde's ass as she walks by.

Sex could be enticing tonight. But then I remember I don't have an actual bed and have been sleeping on a blow-up mattress. I don't need some airhead chick blabbing to the papers about how I live like a weird hermit with no furniture. Fucking just used to be fucking. But now, even trying to get off was more complicated than trigonometry. I had to consider whether or not she'd take pictures of my junk while I was sleeping. If she'd tell people my address. If said girl would become too attached and try to fake a pregnancy or some shit. And these all may sound insane, but if the media training my agent was putting me through taught me anything, it was that people trying to hang on to your fame were insane.

It's in this exact moment that I spot her.

Standing not fifty feet from me, shaking her hips and spilling some pink-colored drink all over her mile-high heels, is Annabelle Mills.

Fucking hell.

She looks edible. I have to sink my teeth into my tongue to keep it from falling out of my head. A skin-tight silver dress that looks like it might slip right over her ass if she bends the wrong way. Legs for days, a waist that begs to be held close. All of that hair, dark and tumbling down her back. I knew from experience that it smelled like caramel and felt like silk running through your fingers.

I can't see them, but those mesmerizing chocolate-hued eyes could hypnotize even the most incredible of magicians.

But that's all it is with Annabelle. Smoke and mirrors. A pretty package. Because everything underneath is rotten, right down to the core.

Who the hell knows how she even got in here, seeing as she wasn't twenty-one yet. Probably had one of those fake IDs from China that all those sorority girls sent away for now, with the real holograms and everything.

Wait ... shit. She is twenty-one. She might be two years younger in terms of school years, but now I remember her birthday. October seventeenth, which makes her old for her grade. Was it weird that I still remember her birthday? Probably. But with my birthday falling late for my grade, making me younger, and hers falling at the top of the educational calendar, I forgot that there weren't as many years between us as I thought.

I hated myself for remembering all of that.

A guy comes up behind her, grabbing her waist and grinding his entire pelvis into her ass. Annabelle backs up into him, shimmying and shaking as she gulps down the mixed drink sloshing out of a plastic cup. It's sloppy and desperate, and I cringe at the sight. For a girl with her brains and looks, she sure has no idea of her worth. She was the same way in high school, always taking whatever attention guys gave her and capitalizing on it.

My hands have begun to shake, and I have to shove them in my pockets in the hopes that Hudson doesn't notice the meltdown happening right next to him.

She's always been able to do this to me. Get my heart racing as if it's sprinting the Kentucky Derby. Just the sight of Annabelle unnerves me, she's my kryptonite. One look at her and I'm cut off at the knees, sputtering, barely breathing.

No person, no woman, should be able to do that to me. That's how I got in trouble last time; because this effect she has on me blinded me. But I won't let it happen now. I will never be that weak, that vulnerable, with her again.

Which is why, the minute her drunken eyes flick over to me and then do a double take, I turn right around and walk out of that bar.

"Can we please wrap this up? I have a textiles class in half an hour."

I tap my mustard yellow flat on the tile floor of the kitchen we're standing in.

"I just can't decide if we should do an open concept with an island, or if we should keep it closed and do stools under the overhanging counter." Ramona taps her chin.

Swiping my finger over the iPad given to me by the showrunners, I present her with the two designs I mocked up in our software. "I think the island makes the most sense in here. It'll create more storage and a better flow, plus you can always put stools on one side."

James gives me a thumbs-up as he passes, a measuring tape in his hand. He's measuring for window treatments, and also trying to hurry Ramona along. She's been more indecisive than usual this morning, and my hangover is barely being restrained on its leash.

I should not have done that final tequila shot last night. Or the three before it. But with my mom-meltdown and Boone back in town ... something feels off. My skin is too itchy; like it shrunk, and I don't fit into it or something. Classes this week have been hell, and the house we are working on for the show is a nightmare. James and the contractor found mold in the basement, so the floor is being ripped up as we speak. I had a ton of shipping disasters with furniture and decor pieces I'd ordered, and on top of that, the slab of granite we picked for the kitchen counters cracked when someone dropped it from the forklift at the warehouse.

So, I'd gone out on a Thursday night. My closest friend in the interior design program, Thea, had badgered me until I'd let her raid my closet and feed me way too many sugary bay breezes. And then one thing had led to another and I practically sprained my ankles dancing on top of a speaker at The Whiskey Room, which was basically just your average disgusting college town bar.

And here we are. Massive hangover that is making my brain vibrate with agony, a boss who won't give it up and just let us go home, and the niggling feeling that I saw a ghost last night.

Because I must have had way too much to drink if I thought I saw Boone at The Whiskey Room.

The guy I'd glimpsed had been more muscular and scruffy than I remembered my high school crush, so maybe it wasn't him. Yet … the way my system had gone on edge at that moment, lighting up like it had been shocked with electricity …

I shake my head, trying to clear the icepick headache from my temple and all thoughts of that stupid guy. "Ramona, I have to go."

My tone is probably a little bit more disrespectful than I mean it to be because my mentor frowns and sets down her tile samples. She leads me, one hand on my back, to a quiet corner of the kitchen away from crew or cameras.

"Honey, are you okay? You've seemed a little on edge this week."

I will never admit it to their faces, but this is another reason why I like my bosses so much. James and Ramona have certainly not let the limelight of their fame taint who they are as people. They're still one hundred percent sweethearts, great parents, and care about the work they do and the people they do it for.

I shrug her off. Feelings are a weakness I can't afford. "I'm fine. Just had too much to drink last night."

Ramona chuckles and tucks my hair behind my ear. "Gosh, do I miss those days sometimes. Be careful though. You're a beautiful girl, but in this day and age, you need to be cautious when you're out at night."

I can't help but crack a smile. Protecting myself against men is the least of my worries. My inner-bitch can scare even the creepiest of males off in three seconds flat.

"I'm always careful. But I do really need to get to class. Do you need me any longer?" I check my phone and see that I'll need to speed to get to my three p.m. lecture.

"No, no, go. Sorry, we're all a bit off today. See you next week. Have a good couple of days off, okay?"

I nod as I speed walk to my car. While I admire James and Ramona, they aren't as shrewd as I am with their business. They give everyone a weekend break every other week. They tailor the show's shooting schedule around the kid's activities and holidays and insist on being home to sit down at dinner with their family every night.

Maybe if I'd had an upbringing like that, I wouldn't be as cold and callous as I am now. But I didn't, and I think it's foolish to give up what extra revenue and projects they could be bringing in if they worked like maniacs. Once I graduate, I plan to work myself into the ground trying to build an enterprise.

I was right. I did have to do ten over the speed limit in my white RAV4 just to make it to campus with barely any time left before my class. As I drag myself into the lecture hall where the course always is, I feel like I might pass out. All I've had today was a protein bar and a Pedialyte when what I really want are a nice, juicy burger and curly fries. My head is pounding, my feet kill from the shoes I danced in last night, and it's so cold outside that my Texas bones are rattling.

"You feel like death, too?" Thea addresses me as I sit next to her in my usual seat, halfway up the stadium-style rows.

"Ugh, yes. And I had to go over to shoot a portion of the show this morning. Remind me never to go out on a Thursday again?"

"Oh, did you guys go to The Whiskey Room last night?" A petite blonde whose name I can't remember interrupts our conversation.

I give her a look that could freeze fire. "Not like it's any of your business, but we did."

She turns immediately back around, but not before I see the hurt on her face.

"Down, girl. Don't be such a bitch," Thea scolds me.

Guilt and disappointment wash over me. I don't mean to be so cold, but it's my nature. I don't know how to change it. I've tried meditation, therapy, kickboxing ... none of it works. My outlook on the world is just negative, and I'm not sure how to undo the parts of my brain that are fucked-up.

"I'm sorry, I didn't mean it." I hope it's loud enough for the blonde to hear, but she doesn't turn back around.

My friend next to me has a concerned look on her face. "Hey, you want to play hooky?"

My hangover agrees immediately, but my inner-perfectionist revolts against the idea. "I don't skip class."

"Come on, you wouldn't be a college student if you didn't, at least once, skip a class. Live a little, Princess Perfect. You're already an on-screen intern for the hottest design show on TV. I think you're light-years ahead of everyone sitting in this lecture hall." Thea rolls her eyes and flicks my arm.

"Ow." I rub the spot, giving her my accurately practiced death stare.

She's kind of right though. Missing this one lecture won't hurt me. I know I was just bitching about how Ramona and James were soft on their hustle, but I was hungover and cranky. And the thought of sitting in Professor Sear's class, listening to her drone on about patterns and swatches, has me grinding my teeth together.

"Fine," I relent. "But we're going for cheeseburgers because I said so."

"Whatever you say, Queen Bee."

6

BOONE

I only have an hour in between my workout and the film session that the hitting coaches want us to attend.

My entire schedule since moving to Austin has been busy as hell and completely out of whack. Between getting my class schedule figured out, sprinting across campus to get to the buildings, dealing with my moving company, figuring out where to park my car in front of my building, practicing with the Triple-A affiliate team I was drafted to and everything in between ... I'm fucking wiped.

I've been scouted for the major leagues since my sophomore year of high school, so I thought I'd been semi-prepared for what was to come, but my mind feels like it has been put in a blender for the last two weeks. I had so not been prepared. It was as if I was hobbling around in the dark in my new reality, trying to grasp at things before they moved on me.

I needed to get it the fuck together. I am a professional now and having a career as a professional baseball player would only get harder from here.

From the few times I'd visited Austin for tournaments or the odd family trip, I remember we'd gone to Big Cheese's Grill.

They boasted the best burgers in town, and it was close enough to campus that the place was always packed with students and professors alike.

I open the door to the restaurant while glancing at my iWatch to check the calories versus fat burned during my workout.

And I slam right into a body.

I bounce back, shocked at the person who just rammed into me. I fumble to hold on to them, to keep our gravity from sending both of us flying. I fail, and the body falls backward, the door slamming into my back. I absorb that blow and keep upright, thank God, or I would have been sprawled flat on top of whoever just plowed into me.

"*Seriously?!* Watch where you're going!" An angry, high-pitched tone fills my ears.

My head is down, trying to collect its scrambled thoughts, as I reach for whoever I just knocked to the ground. "I'm so sorry, I didn't realize you were coming out—"

The air and words leave me as I pull her up. Her hand is still in mine as we stand face-to-face, my surprise mirrored back at me. Those lips, the lashes, the eyes a rich, deep, soul-searching brown. The freckles across the bridge of her nose that make her look more innocent than she actually is.

A current of tension radiates back and forth between our interlocked hands, and I can smell the glass of wine she must have just drunk on her breath. It's sweet with a bite of alcohol, and my mouth waters for a drink. I haven't thirsted for alcohol in five years, yet in one chance meeting, Annabelle has me reaching for a bottle. She's poison to me, makes me want to do crazy things. I drop her hand as the thought crosses my mind, as if she's burned me.

"You should really watch where you're going. Or did you knock me down on purpose?" Annabelle sniffs.

I scoff, "Right, I often go around pushing women to the ground on purpose. I see the cold hard ice hasn't melted off your personality, Annabelle."

And a woman she is. So much more grown up than I remembered her. She'd always been beautiful but gone was the gangliness of teenage years. This is a woman who stands in front of me, curves abound and an unseen knowledge of the world to match. I couldn't help but get that jab in there.

"And I see you're just as focused on yourself as ever. You never did care what anyone else was doing, did you, Boone?" She folds her arms over her chest and my eyes stray to her boobs in a sizzle of heat between us.

We're like a bunch of children fighting like cats and dogs out in the street. How can she still pull out every insecure and immature trait within me? My brain is moving seconds slower than it usually does, and I know I'm standing here staring too long. Even though I hate Annabelle Mills, I can't help but memorize every detail about her for the first time I've seen her in about five years.

"Move." Annabelle pushes past me, not using any manners, and starts to stalk down the sidewalk.

Talk about rude. She'd always been aggressive, harsh, and just a little bit more high-maintenance than any of the other girls. It's what had drawn me to her. And then seeing those glimpses of vulnerability, that's what had made me stay. It was addicting feeling like you were the only one who got to see the nice side of the mean girl.

I should walk into the restaurant. I should pick up my to-go order and drive back to my apartment where I'll eat a quick lunch and change and go to the practice facility.

But a flash of Annabelle in the bar the other night dances through my head. And her callous words just now piss me off even more.

She always did have the perfect way of getting under my skin and driving me wild. When I'm around her, I forget who I am. I turn into some raging bull, with a fuse shorter than the bombs Itchy and Scratchy use on each other.

The stupidest thing I could do right now? Stomp after her, yelling, in the middle of a crowded downtown street.

So that's exactly what I do.

"You really haven't changed a bit!" Oh, fuck. What am I doing?

Annabelle rolls around, her eyes sparking with rage. "Nope, still the same cold, heartless bitch you dumped."

"Yeah, like I said, I can see that." Lord, my mama would be so disappointed in me agreeing with a woman that she was a bitch.

"Well, no one said you had to be around it. You're the one who moved to my city. You're welcome to leave." She waves around like I should just get out of here.

I fist my hands in my hair. Christ, she's so aggravating. "No can do, I'm getting paid to be here."

She rolls her eyes. "Like I'm not? Have you watched TV lately? Or did you take one too many fly balls to the head? I know there weren't a lot of brain cells in there to start."

Fuck her. Now it's time to really piss her off, get under her skin like she's under mine. "Oh, you mean that show you play house on or whatever? They'll get bored of you when the next eye-candy pageant queen comes along."

I swear Annabelle could spit nails at me if she willed it right now. "You're an asshole, Boone Graham. You've only ever cared about yourself and where you want to be. It was silly of me to think you'd ever think of someone but yourself."

I drop the anvil. "Says the girl who cheated on me. Who lost her virginity to another guy."

People around us are starting to stare, to really look at the two people arguing openly on the street. It's not a good idea for me to stick around any longer; people know who I am on a national level and being seen fighting with a girl, who someone will inevitably social media stalk and find out is my ex, is not good publicity.

Except I can't stop staring into Annabelle's eyes. They are furious, yes, but there is something more there. I've really ... hurt her. I'm shocked, to be honest. I didn't think I could remotely hurt this girl, who self-identifies as a cold, heartless bitch.

But there it is. The raw flash, miss-it-if-you-blink second of real pain that flickers through those mocha pools. I open my mouth to say something, to take it back, maybe apologize, but she speaks first.

"You have no idea."

Her tone pulls at my heartstrings, it's low and somber. And then she melts into the crowd, giving no explanation of what I have no idea about.

7

ANNABELLE

I remember that day on the front steps of the high school as if it just happened an hour ago.

My heart had been in my throat, ascending them that morning. I'd royally messed up the Saturday night before, and I knew that the rumor of Cain and I having sex was making its way around the student body.

Except, it wasn't a rumor. It was true.

Boone had been away for a baseball tournament that weekend, and I hadn't seen him since Friday when he'd kissed me goodbye in the exact same spot. I'd reveled in that kiss, his hand on the back of my neck, the passionate push of his tongue into my mouth. I'd beamed at the fact that a senior boy was kissing me, a sophomore girl, in front all the world to see. It felt exciting, I felt popular, but most of all … I just really loved kissing Boone.

But now, all I felt as I walked up to him on those steps Monday morning was sheer dread. Because after this conversation, he was not going to kiss me anymore. He wasn't going to want anything to do with me.

He was going to hate me.

I remember him grabbing my elbow to pull me toward a

quieter part of the stairs, but it didn't matter. Everyone was watching us.

I remember how Boone was barely able to look at me. How he grunted out questions and made non-committal answers as I stared down at my shoes answering him, admitting to my mistake, as I tried not to cry.

I remember how, for the briefest of seconds, he looked like he might reach out and touch my cheek. How hope had sparked in my chest, like a small flame that grew higher as the moment stretched on, my teenage delusion leading me on.

And I remember the words that were seared into my memory when he spoke.

"You are a disgusting person. I want nothing to do with you. We are done."

I was devastated. In myself. In him. In the whole situation.

That feeling, that raw ache, like the burn of acid reflux that never goes away, corrodes my chest even now. I sit in my car, trying to breathe in and out, after our confrontation on the street.

I wish that I'd just left with Thea. If I hadn't stayed to use the bathroom, if I'd left the restaurant just three minutes earlier, I would have avoided running into Boone. I could have stayed blissfully ignorant about his presence in Austin.

But no, I'd run right into him. Literally, smack into that mass of muscles that had only gotten more manly and handsome since the last time I'd seen him. God, that body. Arms and legs like tree trunks, a torso molded of steel. That auburn hair, with a tinge of red, as if he was a Viking king.

It was the eyes, though. Always the eyes that got me. See, Boone was a quiet one. He was the type of guy who didn't say much until you really got to know him. And so, his eyes said what his mouth didn't.

Honey brown, almost caramel. They were seductive and

piercing, with flecks of gold. God, I could get lost in those eyes. I used to get lost in those eyes.

Although, today, he'd seemed to have a lot to say. Clearly, he still hated me. It wasn't as if I hadn't expected that, but ... God.

Boone was so angry. I could feel the rage boiling under his skin.

And I might have told him I was a heartless bitch, but that was obviously a lie. Or else I wouldn't be crying in my car right now at his words that barbed my skin like the sharpest wire. He'd held up the mirror straight to my face and shown me just how ugly I was.

I haven't had to deal much with what I did to him. In a matter of seconds, it had been over between us. Yes, I'd been upset and heartbroken, but I'd never had to unpack why I cheated or how it killed a small piece of my soul. And now, all these years later, all of that emotional baggage has been heaped upon me in the middle of downtown Austin.

He'd never understand why I had slept with Cain. He'd never seen me, he'd never expressed that I truly meant anything to him. I was fresh meat to whet his appetite, one who he could leave without a backward glance when he went off to college. Boone and I's relationship had been spiraling by the time I'd gone into the woods with Cain at that bonfire party. Of course, alcohol was a big contributor to that night, but the same old insecurity that had always haunted me took hold as the night went on.

Boone went out of town for a tournament. He hadn't texted or called me in approximately thirty-six hours, even though I'd been desperate and texted him three times in a row without a response. I was a girl who'd been left by the one person in my life who was supposed to love me unconditionally, so it wasn't a mystery that I freaked out when I felt like someone was leaving me behind again. It didn't help that in a matter of months, he actually would be leaving me behind. It also didn't help that we'd been together for a few months and Boone had never once called me his girlfriend.

I didn't matter to him. I was replaceable, easily forgettable.

So I did the most catastrophic thing I could to get attention. To hurt the way I was hurting. To make him angry enough to react.

That's what I remembered most about our breakup on the school's front steps.

He'd looked so angry, I could practically taste the fury coming off of him.

I wasn't angry. I was hurt.

Devastated, actually.

Not only had she cheated on me, but she'd given her virginity to someone else. Not that we were anywhere near sex, we'd only be seeing each other for a couple of months, but it was the principle of it. To me, the fact that she was a virgin had been kind of sacred. Or as sacred as it could have been to a teenage boy.

I had already had sex, with two different girls. But I'd really liked Annabelle. I was half in love with her, again, in that teenage boy kind of way where love feels like it's swallowing you whole.

That morning on the steps, I'd barely been able to speak for the fear of exploding on her. I wanted to take my fist to Cain Kent's face, I wanted to smash in Annabelle's locker. I wanted to do anything to hurt her as badly as I was hurting at that moment.

I might not have shown it so much, I was quiet compared to my egotistical peers and so focused on baseball that maybe I let my feelings take a back seat ... but I really liked Annabelle. It hadn't just been the type of crush that a senior has on a younger girl simply because she was fresh meat. No, I'd genuinely liked her. We hung out alone together, I brought her to parties as my girl, we'd gone to homecoming together. She met my parents and I'd actually gone fishing with her dad one morning.

I probably should have moved quicker on the asking her to officially be my girlfriend front, but for all intents and purposes, we were already there.

And then she went and fucked it all up.

I remember getting the texts after I turned my phone back on. It died halfway through Saturday at the tournament and I'd forgotten a charger. Someone loaned me one on the bus on the way home, and my cell had lit up with dozens of messages.

A couple were from Annabelle, and they became angrier and more sloppy as I scrolled down. Shit, I was an idiot. I'd gone away and hadn't once texted her. And now she was probably drunk, at the weekly bonfire. I texted her back before looking at any of the messages.

Boone: *I'm sorry, babe. My phone died. I'm coming right to you the minute the bus gets back.*

Which would probably be one a.m. Sunday morning, but I could always climb through her window. I'd done it before.

And then I opened the other messages.

A sick, sour feeling crept up along the back of my neck and took hold of my throat as I read texts from two of my buddies on the football team. In a nutshell, they were reaching out to tell me that my girl had fucked that new quarterback, kid with the last name Kent.

Kenzie, a girl I'd hooked up with last year, had sent a grainy picture of Annabelle and this kid standing by the fire, but that proved nothing.

It was only when I read the text from one of my best friends, Jeremy, that I knew it had to be true.

Jeremy: *Dude, hate to be the one to tell you this ... but, I saw Annabelle making out with that new sophomore quarterback. I'm sorry, man.*

I had to control myself from throwing my phone against the window. Or crushing it in my fist. The poison of rage started to sprint along my veins, coursing through me until I was one big, hot ball of fury.

How dare she?

I put a steadying hand on the seat in front of me and looked around, wondering if any of the other guys on the travel team, those who attended Haven High, knew what my girl had done tonight.

But ... maybe it was all a misunderstanding. Maybe she was drunk, and he took advantage of her. Then I'd really kill him. Or maybe the people who were at the party just didn't realize the situation.

I could talk to her. We could figure it out.

I read Jeremy's text again and knew. No ... we were not going to figure this out.

I remember stomping up those front steps at school, waiting for her.

I remember people staring as she walked up to me.

I remember her answers, short and cold and to the point. Did she even care that what we had was over?

Did she even care how much she'd hurt me?

After I'd dumped her on that morning, I barely saw her the rest of the school year. I kept my distance, except for the bonfire where I'd punched Cain Kent in the face. Twice. I made it known that she wasn't to come to the parties I was at and to leave my group of friends alone.

I went to prom with another girl and fucked a different one at the lake cabin we rented for prom weekend. I graduated and went on with my life, packing away the heartache for Annabelle in a small recess of that organ that stopped beating in my chest. I never dated another person, just had the occasional one-night stand.

Honestly, I would have been just fine on my own. I would play the game I love, travel the world, and do what I pleased with no strings attached.

If I'd never run into Annabelle Mills outside that restaurant, I would never have to think about my stupid, fucking heart again.

Hey Annabelle!

I hope your week is going well! I wanted to say that I loved that pink suede couch you picked out on last week's episode.

Mr. Kutch wanted to know if you would be able to make a meeting with him in the next few weeks to discuss something?

Let me know,

Mallory Hues

Executive Assistant to Kenneth Kutch, CEO of the Flipping Channel

I'm mildly shocked when I open up my email halfway through the school week. I have a university email which is reserved for classes and professors, and a personal email for all of my *Hart & Home* business.

The personal one is a certified mess. I may be good at design and decor, and even handling people most days, but organization is definitely not my strong suit. Nothing is sorted by folders; vendor emails are mixed in with invoices from furniture designers and marble warehouses. And there are about fifty unread messages somewhere in the pages and pages of emails I haven't deleted, and I'm too lazy to find them and read them.

So it's weird when I open a message from Mallory, the assistant to the channel's CEO. She's always been kind to me when we've had to communicate, but I wonder why she's emailing now. I wonder what Kenneth Kutch wants to speak to me about.

Maybe they want to give me my own show.

I think the thought, and then think about how crazy and egotistical I am to even consider this as a possibility. But then, I take the thoughts or irrationality back, because I know I could have my own show. How ready I am to stop living on the outskirts of Ramona and James' show.

I know how lucky I am. How jealous people are. The shit they say behind my back, that I must be blowing a producer or having threesomes with James and Ramona. I am aware of how truly insane it is that a random college intern is now on one of the most popular TV shows in the United States.

But ... at the same time, it's not insane. Have you ever seen those interviews with celebrities or D-list celebs, like the Real Housewives, when they say that they just always knew they were going to be famous?

That's how I felt. How I feel.

That may sound conceited, but it's true. From a young age, I knew I was supposed to be in the limelight. At first, I didn't understand the buzz around me, why people always wanted to do what I was doing or be close to me. But over time, I saw the power I could yield. And now I understand that that power, that control, and presence I command, has propelled me to the place I always wanted to get to.

So no, I'm not surprised that the channel executives want to have a meeting with me. I am confident and self-assured, which most women like to tear other women down for. Why do we do that? It's okay to know that you're kick-ass at what you do. It's more than okay to be sure in your heart and mind that you'll succeed and adopt a take-no-prisoners attitude while trying to do that.

Some might call me a bitch for that. I call it ambitious.

After catching up on some other emails, I pack my laptop into my school bag and change into workout clothes. Every Monday, Wednesday and Friday, I hit the fitness center before class to get my cardio and weights in. Running is a stress relief for me, and if you add in some pump-up country music at full blast, I'm sometimes blessed enough to stop hearing my own thoughts for five minutes.

I text Harper before I leave my dorm room to see if she wants to meet me there.

Harper: *Cain isn't training at the Athletics Center today, so he's tagging along. See you in ten.*

Annabelle: *Yay, third wheel status. As usual.*

Harper: *Don't act as if you really want a wheel so that we could double date. You've flattened every wheel we've tried to set you up with.*

I have to chuckle to myself as I walk down the last set of stairs in my dorm building and out into the chilly campus air. I wrap my scarf tighter around my neck and curse myself for wearing workout pants with mesh stripes down the calves. My poor legs are freezing.

Harper is right, though. Three times, she and Cain have tried to set me up with one of his friends from class or the football team. And all three times, I've been a complete asshole on the dates. The guys were either too boring, too egotistical, or too ... well, I don't mean to be mean, but dumb. Oh all right, I do mean to be mean.

I'm just picky when it comes to guys. Which is usually why I'd rather kiss them than talk to them. I may not be my roommate, who should host a Dr. Ruth-type show on the campus TV station, but I've had my fair share of one-night stands. All I want is a release. In that moment, sex is not a vulnerability. I'm not showing love to that other person. I'm using them for a couple of blissful seconds of orgasm, and then I want them to get out of my bed.

It's probably a harsh truth, but it's mine. I just don't want that connection. It's distracting, and no one has caught my eye in that way since Boone. And look how royally I screwed that one up. No, I was glad to stay the third wheel.

Harper and Cain walk toward me where I stand at the entrance to the fitness center, their hands interlocked, and I roll my eyes.

"Please no making out on the treadmill," I say in greeting.

Harper laughs. "Of course we wouldn't do that. I can't stand the couples who kiss between every chest press."

Cain raises his eyebrows. "I can promise that. I can't promise we won't have sex in the locker room."

I make a gagging noise and Harper pushes him. "Gross. I won't even go in there without flip-flops. I'd never have sex in there."

"I think I can convince you." He grabs her waist and squeezes, tickling her.

I feel his presence before I turn around and see him. Isn't that weird? How attuned you can be to a person without having seen them in years? The hair on my arms sticks up, and the cold air around me becomes charged with heat. Even though it's the middle of winter, I begin to sweat.

"Figures you're still with this guy."

Boone's voice is deep and threatening, his eyes glued in disgust to Cain.

I think I'm so shocked to see him on campus, that I don't even think about him and Cain being in the same airspace. "What are you doing here? You can't use these facilities, they're for students."

Those whiskey-colored eyes are flinty as they flick to me. "And I'm a student. So what, you're with this asshole?"

Cain smirks. "This asshole is definitely taken."

He's toying with Boone, just for a rise. He's lucky if he doesn't get punched in the face again. I can hear Cain grind his teeth.

Harper is naïve to the situation. She raises a hand in greeting. "Uh hi, Harper. Taker of this asshole."

Boone shakes his head as if to clear it, trying to work out the situation. "You are the one he's with?"

I butt in. "You attend college here? What ... why?"

I'm so confused. He signed a major league contract. He's due to start for the Triple AAA team in Austin (okay, so I googled his deal). Why would he be going to college?

And then my brain starts whooping out alert bells and whistles. He can't go here. I can't be forced to see him every day on campus for who knows how long. It was bad enough when we attended the same high school for a couple of months after he'd dumped me. But having to run into him awkwardly years later? My body shudders at the tension of it all.

Harper smiles, finally figuring out who he is. "Ah, you must be the infamous Boone. Yes, I'm this asshole's girlfriend. I love him, but good job punching younger Cain in the face. He was a real prick when I met him."

"Hey!" Cain reacts to her joking insult.

Harper continues. "It's a fucked-up situation, to be honest. Annabelle is my stepsister, who also happens to have slept with my boyfriend, but you already knew that. It was before I met either of them, though. And Cain became my boyfriend before my mom married Annabelle's dad, so it's not as weird as you think."

I want to walk away from this conversation. I'm mortified from all of this tea being spilled, and jumpy as all hell having Boone standing just feet from me. Dripping in sweat, did I mention he was dripping in sweat? And despite it being cold as the North Pole, we Texas girls didn't have a thick skin for winter, he's only wearing workout shorts and a skin-tight Under Armor T-shirt. I have to actually tighten my thigh muscles to keep from rubbing my legs together.

"No, it sounds pretty fucked-up." A small smile ghosts Boone's lips, and my mouth goes dry.

How can I loathe this man but also want to see him naked all at the same time?

How can I loathe this woman but also want to see her naked all at the same time?

I can't stop staring at Annabelle's side profile, especially the lower half of her that is clad in those skin-tight black leggings that the entire female population of the world seems to own these days. Those black leggings will be the death of men, I swear.

"Hey man, listen, I hope the best for you in the pros. And, no hard feelings." That asshole Cain Kent holds his hand out to me.

He wants me to shake his hand, like a man. I search inside and find that I really don't hold a grudge against him. Plus, his girlfriend and Annabelle's stepsister is actually kind of funny, in the couple of minutes I've known her, so maybe he has changed.

I reach out and take his hand, shaking it. "Yeah, thanks."

For a second after we have our tender bro moment, the awkward silence penetrates the air.

And then Harper speaks. "Well, we are off to work out. See you in there, Annabelle."

She drags Cain away, leaving a pissed off and gaping-mouthed Annabelle standing in front of me. Her eyes are throwing daggers at her retreating friends' backs, and then she turns to me.

"Seriously? You can just forgive him, but you got into a shouting match with me on the street the other day? And you go here? You can't be a student here."

I chuckle. "Always telling people what they can and can't do. I am a student here. I want to get a degree. I'm not just some caveman baseball player, unlike what you may think about me. And yeah, I can forgive that guy. There really isn't anything to forgive him for, honestly. We aren't going to be friends, but I don't hold anything against him. He wasn't the one who cheated on me."

I had to shove it in her face again because the wound she'd left in my heart still hadn't scabbed over all the way.

"I get it, Boone. You hate me. I'm not your biggest fan either, so just stay away from me and I'll stay away from you."

Her admission reminds me of her words on the sidewalk by the Big Cheese that day. "What did I ever do to you?"

I want to rile her up. I want some kind of actual emotion from this cold robot-woman who never let me completely in. "I'll avoid you, you avoid me."

Annabelle dodges the question and skitters away into the fitness center. She's running scared, I'm just not sure why. And I'm reminded that it's going to be very hard to avoid her. Sure, our college campus is big, but its fate's cruel joke that we've run into each other twice in two weeks in a city of more than a million people. It's going to happen again. I could avoid her at the gym, though. Today, I'd just gone to get a change of scenery for my workout. Students here didn't recognize me as much as someone would at the team's practice facility, which usually featured reporters here and there.

I'm not crazy enough, today at least, to go after her. But something in me wants to. What the hell is wrong with me? I came here to do two things. Earn my college degree and kick-start my professional baseball career. I have no time for women, especially those who broke my damn heart.

I need to get a damn grip.

Baseball, baseball, just think about baseball.

From the time I could hold a whiffle ball bat, I knew that baseball would be it for me.

The strategy, the superstition, the quiet, steady rhythm of the game ... it all intrigued me. I would stay up late at night reading the backs of baseball cards, memorizing stats and facts about the game's most famous players through its history.

When I was about twelve, I'd been at a clinic for hitting and fielding. Back then, my parents and I had thought it was just a hobby. Something I was good at and could probably make the high school team when I got there, but nothing super serious.

And that's when it happened. Something fell into place in my mind, and I began hitting every single softball pitch they threw to me over the fence of the little league park. Some local travel team coaches had been in attendance and had approached my mom and dad about getting me onto their roster.

From there, it escalated quickly. I practiced twenty hours a week year round. There were private lessons and professionally fitted gloves. I traveled every weekend from February to August for tournaments. The press started wanting to talk to me. Mom started clipping newspaper articles and making an album of my accomplishments. Our travel team won State. Dad began putting together highlight reels from my high school games since I'd made varsity as a freshman. Then scouts started approaching me at games, telling me how much so-and-so college would love for me to be a part of their program.

This was my ticket. This was our ticket.

It wasn't that I grew up poor, but the Grahams definitely

weren't the wealthiest people in Haven. Both of my parents had jobs, and they kept food on the table and the heat on in the winter ... but there wasn't much left over. I wore clothes from Walmart or Goodwill, I saved up years' worth of birthday money for the clunker of a truck I drove once I got my license.

And especially now, with what's been going on at home for years ... we need it more than ever. I still needed to sit down with my agent and the team to hammer out my rookie contract, but once I had that money, I'd be sending a chunk of it home for Mom.

And hope to God that she didn't use it to enable Dad.

I started the SUV I'd rented since moving here, someday I'd get around to buying something, and drove back to my apartment. Downtown Austin was buzzing on this weekday, and it took me twice as long as it would have to get home when I was at my original college choice in Pennsylvania.

Austin was in Texas, and it was a city, but it pretty much qualified as its own brand of Country with a capital C. Sure, people here still listened to Blake Shelton and Carrie Underwood, but I mention the younger country stars because that's what this place is. Young. It's a living, breathing millennial hub, with tech companies and liberalism weaved into the old Texas ways. There is both a shop for cowboy boots and a vegan taco counter on my block.

I'm enjoying the city and am more surprised that I enjoy being back in my home state.

But I need to stay focused. I need to become a drill sergeant about dedicating myself to my sport. And the only other thing that I can let be a distraction are classes.

There is no room for Annabelle Mills and her drama in my agenda.

"Let's go up and introduce ourselves."

James is acting like a giddy schoolboy and I could slap him right now.

I rode back from the country house we'd been working on all day with him and Ramona. They said we needed to have a design meeting, and no better way to kill two birds with one stone than by using the hour commute back to the city to have that discussion.

In the car, we'd talked about the paint colors for the dining room, whether or not James was going to put wainscoting on the hallway stairs, and if we could afford a new sectional and still be on budget for our clients.

And by the time I looked up, I thought we'd be outside of my dorm, where they'd dropped me dozens of times.

Instead, I found myself at a fan appreciation day for the Austin farm team that Boone had been drafted to.

I could kill these two right now, I swear.

"Oh, honey, you're like a darn child, I swear," Ramona twanged and smiled.

I was trying to be invisible, sink into the ground or blend

into the bleachers or something. I should have just stayed in the car, feigning a headache or something so that they would hurry this up. But they caught me off guard, suggesting we go in to see the rookie, Boone Graham. As if I'd had a choice, James had already parked the truck and was halfway across the parking lot before I blew out a frustrated breath.

We were behind the fence of a practice baseball field, the chain link reaching high into the sky. I think this facility was supposed to appear like a little league field, except that it was so state-of-the-art, they weren't fooling anybody. Perfectly manicured grass, the cement bowl of a stadium behind us, with red and gray seats for fans to watch from. There were professional food vendors up on the top tier, and even a wall in the outfield modeled after the Green Monster. Yes, I might be a fashion-loving home decor nut, but I know a little bit about baseball.

When Boone and I had been together, it hadn't been baseball season. I'd never gotten to wear his jersey and sit in the stands, cheering when he hit a home run. Being here, in the state that we were in, is weird. But also intimate. I could feel him in every part of this sport. The slow, deliberate nature of it. The quiet process of strategy. The way that it was both relaxed and completely on edge all at the same time.

"Look, he's coming over! BOONE! SIGN MY HAT!" James took his ball cap off his head and swung it above him like a crazy person.

People were looking now, pointing out that James Hart was here, and he wanted to meet the rookie. Honestly, James and Ramona were probably bigger draws here than any of the players.

Boone begins slowly moseying over with some of his teammates to say hi to the celebrities who'd come to see him practice, and I want to melt into the dirt beneath my feet.

Ramona leans over and whispers, "Oh, Anna, look how cute he is. I swear if I was twenty years younger ..."

You're not kidding, sister, I thought.

And cute would not be the word I would use. It was the pants, those goddamn baseball pants. Tight, white and plastered to his carved thigh muscles, I bet the view from the back looks even better. His forearms are covered in mud, his shirt in dust, and sweat trickles from his temples.

Boone looks like some kind of porno fantasy, and I have to bite down on my tongue to keep from panting.

Why did the guy I was supposed to hate have to be so freaking hot?

He hasn't seen me yet, and I half-hide behind Ramona as they come up to the chain-link fence.

"What're you doing?" She swats at me, annoyed as I try to cling to her back.

"Hey, man, thanks for coming out."

I hear the gruffness of Boone's voice as he walks around the fence, and from my half hidden view, with all of my hair thrust over my face as if that'll keep him from recognizing me, I see him extend a hand to James.

"We're just happier than pigs in shit to welcome you back to Texas. You're going to be a hell of a player for our boys in the big leagues someday." James is like the mascot of the cowboy boots and big hair parade.

"Oh, well, that's sure nice of you to say. I just hope I can live up to all the expectations."

Ramona steps toward him, shaking his hand and revealing me. "Oh, don't listen to him. You'll do just fine, darlin'."

But Boone is staring at me. He's not exactly annoyed, although there is some flintiness to his eyes. No, I think he's more amused at me trying to hide behind Ramona's leg like a five-year-old.

"Annabelle ... didn't think you liked baseball all that much." He smiles sarcastically at me.

My stomach drops, because he's revealed that we know each other. And when a cute boy shows any kind of interest in me in front of Ramona, she starts planning showers and weddings.

"Oh, I didn't realize you two know each other." She smacks her hands together and gives me a you've-got-some-explaining-to-do look.

Before I can talk, Boone cuts me off. "We went to high school together."

James' mouth drops open. "Bells, you didn't want to mention that? Jeez, I've only been talking about the guy for weeks!"

He always calls me this nickname, even though I've told him I hate it. "Must've slipped my mind."

Boone narrows his eyes, and Ramona has this look on her face that I know is just downright bad.

"Say, we have to go to this meeting and don't have time to drop Annabelle off at her dorm. Boone, do you think you could do us a favor? If it's not too much trouble? It'll give you two some time to catch up."

Oh, no she didn't. "No, really, that's okay. I can call a cab."

"Now, Boone, you wouldn't make this girl take a cab, would you?" James seems to be backing his wife's idea, and even winks at me.

I am so enraged that I swear, my head is about to pop off and start whistling like a scalding hot teakettle.

Boone must be stuck between a rock and a hard place, having these influencers in Texas tell him to take me home. I can tell he doesn't want to, even shoots me a dirty look like this was my idea, but that if he doesn't, these two local celebrities might tell people he refused.

"Sure, fine. I'll be back to take you home," Boone grumbles and walks off, his entire mood shifting.

"Great, we'll call you tomorrow!" Ramona singsongs and hugs me, hauling James off before I can rip them both a new one.

Then it hits me.

I'm going to have to sit in Boone's car, alone, for half an hour.

What the hell have my bosses gotten me into?

"I swear, I didn't come here of my own volition."

I make a conscious effort to sit up straight as if this will help protect my head and heart from the panic attack threatening to melt them down.

I've been sitting in a stadium seat for the last half an hour, alone, while Boone went to shower in the locker room. I could kill Ramona for leaving me here to live out her diabolical plan. I've nearly gotten up and left numerous times, but the stadium is in the middle of nowhere and it's an awkward time to catch an Uber. Plus, it's getting late and I'm not stupid enough to stand out in the streets in a part of town I don't really know.

I watch those *Dateline* shows.

"If I was dumb, which you clearly think I am, I would almost believe that." Boone stands above me, changed into blue jeans and a maroon T-shirt, his brown hair freshly washed.

He smells like leather and cinnamon, and I'm surprised to realize that he wears the same cologne he did all those years ago when we'd been together.

I cross my arms over my chest, my inner-evil twin wanting so badly to come out and play. "And if I was dumb, which clearly

I'm not, I would have come here to actually see you. But, like I said, I didn't. I was dragged here by my bosses. I have absolutely no interest in a sport where grown men stand out in a bug-infested field trying to catch a ball."

We stare each other down for what feels like a month until I blink and look away first. His gaze directly on me is unnerving.

Boone sits down next to me, sighing. "Someone up there in the universe wants us to talk, I suppose."

I shuffle my shoes on the concrete stadium row.

"We don't even know each other anymore. There is nothing to talk about." I huff.

Boone eyes me, a small smile playing at his lips. "Don't tell me there is nothing still between us, Annabelle. Even if we don't want it, there is still a spark. There is animosity, there is ... something."

I dare to look at him. "You're right, I don't want this. We barely knew each other back then, we were just stupid high school kids. You don't know me now. I don't know you."

I didn't understand what there was to talk about. Couldn't he just take me home? I don't want to be mature and have closure, not with him. Not when he is trying to make me admit that there is something between us. Because obviously there is, it's like a damn inferno between us. But I couldn't let him see that he was getting to me, just like he had always gotten to me ever since the day I laid eyes on him when I was sixteen.

"I do know you," Boone says quietly.

I can't help it, I fully look at him now. The side of his face, speckled with stubble, those long eyelashes looking straight forward.

"What do you know about me?" I find that I'm breathless.

Boone takes a deep breath.

"You're drama, Annabelle. You think everyone is going to leave you, so you push them to the limits of destruction to see if they'll blow up at you. And me? I'm not into that. I didn't need to declare my love for you after two days together, and you couldn't stand it."

That's really all he thinks of me? The hope that had blossomed in my chest in thinking he might confess how incredible he thinks I am is extinguished so quickly that I might have whiplash. Even though I should harness my inner mature woman, I can't. My blood is beginning to boil at his assumption about me. But especially at his last statement, that I wanted him to ... what? Be my knight in shining armor? *Please*.

"No, what I couldn't stand was that you wouldn't even acknowledge that I did mean something to you! Boone, you couldn't tell me that you cared for me. You were always so wrapped up in *you*, that you barely saw *me*."

The floodgates are going to open. If the universe wanted us to get it all out, here they have it.

He shakes his head. "That's not true at all. I saw you. I've always seen you. Christ, Anna, it's impossible not to see you. You're radiant; the word beautiful was created specifically to describe you."

We both fall silent for a moment, our ragged breaths mingling in the air. I can't tell if he's going to bury his hands in my hair and kiss me or turn around and run away as fast as he can.

"But there is much more than attraction that makes up a relationship. Compromise, support, kindness, humor, compassion ... you don't possess those, Anna. Or at least, I never saw that. Admit it, you liked me half as much as you did because I was a popular senior."

I make a noise, non-committal, as his words sting my soul. One I didn't realize was still in there.

"Maybe. But I also really admired you. I liked you. I felt inferior and invisible when I was with you. So don't accuse me of not having those things for you. Because you weren't bringing them to the table either."

That sharp jaw tilts; regards me. His eyes, shiny as two round copper pennies, hold sadness.

"Seems like we both made a mess of each other."

I was about to make a bigger one. Because we were both sad. And something was happening inside of me that I had ... never felt. A softening, a giving way. My heart cracked open and began to bleed, filling me with the hurt and sorrow I hadn't allowed myself to feel in years. Maybe even my entire life.

Maybe he was right. Maybe I brought drama upon myself. Maybe my life was destined to feature catastrophes akin to a soap opera. Because I was about to give him a scene-stopper.

I lean forward, the arm of the plastic seat separating us. Boone doesn't move, just watches me carefully as I move, inch-by-inch, closer to him. The minute my fingers tentatively brush his arm, resting on the metal division between us, I get spooked.

I move quickly, no time for thought, and lean forward, crushing my lips to his.

But once I get there, I, again, panic. I wasn't smooth or teasing or effortlessly sexy like I'd always dreamed I'd be if I ever got the chance to kiss Boone again. Because as much as I said I hated him, of course, I wanted one last chance to prove how irresistible I am.

I just sit there, my mouth on his, unmoving. It's awkward and weird, with nauseous, nervous energy pulsing in my stomach. *Move, you idiot*, my brain tells me.

Luckily, Boone makes a humming noise that I feel all the way to my toes, and it spurs me to act. I tilt my head, cup his jaw, and begin the mechanics of a kiss. Just like the ones I'd performed time and time again with guys.

But this is nothing like those other times. Because as I begin to finally kiss my ex, the man whose heart I broke ... he begins to kiss me.

Lord have mercy, Boone Graham has learned a few things since high school.

I may have started this, but he is going to finish it. Boone grabs my cheeks, not hard but in a forceful enough way that lets me know he is the one in control now. I scrape my teeth against his bottom lip to let him know he's not the alpha. I am.

That only spurs him on, thrusting his tongue into my mouth and lapping at mine. It's dirty and exploring and it makes me want that tongue down in the lowest, deepest parts of me.

I shouldn't have done it. I shouldn't have acted irrationally or crazily, just like he said was my nature, basically. I'd proved him right, because here we are, going at each other in a place I claimed not having wanted to step foot in.

But ... I wanted to know. I wanted to kiss his lips again and know that I didn't need them to feel something. Because I'd always had this hunch that if we met again, that spark would still be there. I had this hunch that the reason I hadn't been able to feel that spark with anyone else was because I didn't have closure with Boone. If I could get the spark back from him, keep it for myself, give it to someone else ... I could finally let this go.

I was wrong, though. I couldn't get that spark back. It was firmly cemented, right here between us, just like the arm of the seat digging into my ribs.

And I didn't need that kiss to feel something.

I needed it to feel everything. I needed Boone to feel *alive*.

13

I'm at batting practice a few days later, and I still can't get the disgusted expression of Annabelle's face after she pushed me away out of my head.

She'd stopped our kiss, looked like she'd eaten bad fish, and demanded I take her home. Just like I'd said, the girl was nothing but drama.

I was so fucking pissed at myself for touching her. For allowing her to mess with my head like that. I had zero trust in this person, and yet ...

The things she'd said about me only focusing on myself, about not expressing how I felt about her ... I hate to admit it, but she was right. I'd bagged the hot sophomore, I'd done almost the same thing I'd accused her of. I'd been more into what it would look like being with Annabelle than I had about actually *being* with Annabelle.

Underneath all of that steel, bitchy exterior was a vulnerability. She'd let me in just a fraction before she'd slammed the door shut, but she let me know that she'd been hurt by our breakup as well. Really, she'd felt neglected way before she ever hooked up with Cain ... or at least that's how I read her outburst at the practice facility.

"Dude, that was a softball, pay attention!"

Hudson throws me a what-the-fuck hand gesture from behind the batting screen he's been pitching balls from. We're mostly here by ourselves, except for the guys milling in and out of the weight room. He, like me, doesn't take days off. If we don't have practice or film or media, and I don't have school, I'm still here working on my swing or doing catching drills.

"Sorry, man, my head was just somewhere else." I shake it off, getting back into my stance.

But Hudson is already walking toward me. "What's up? Hmm, let me guess. Girl troubles?"

I'm a little surprised. "How did you know that?"

"You might be a quiet guy, but your brooding can't be mistaken. That's chick sulking, dude."

"Chick sulking?" I chuckle.

"You've got that frown that says 'some woman just fucked me up sideways and I'm not sure how to feel about it.'"

"I didn't know that was a thing. But I guess ... that's pretty accurate." I shrug.

"What did she do?" Hudson juggles two baseballs around and around in his hands.

I give him the long and short of it. "Cheated on me in high school, and then kissed me a few days ago."

He snorts. "Well, shit, man, sounds like you got a lot of girl troubles."

"Tell me about it. She's the devil. I hate her."

"Except you don't." He eyes me knowingly.

Fuck. I do, and I don't. I hate how she betrayed me, how she gave it up to someone else. That I wasn't the first ... as male and chauvinistic as that sounds. I hate that she's so smug and confident, but I also love it. I love her ice and that she's a bit damaged, just like me. We wore our baggage like medals of honor. Annabelle was addicting, and even if I hated her, I also didn't.

"Should we get back to it?" I clear my throat.

Hudson nods, knowing I am done talking about my chick sulking and walks back to the mound. Pitch after pitch comes soaring at me, and I crack each one off of my favorite batting practice bat.

I have a lucky game bat, my favorite practice one, ones that I'll settle for as backups, and other brands that I will not even touch. Baseball is nothing if not a game of superstition.

Hearing that *thwack*, feeling the reverberations of the hit travel through my hands and down my spine and suffuse in my blood, it's a rush of adrenaline I'll never be able to fully explain to those who have never felt it. It's raw, almost sexual. It gets my engine revving, it's primal. To know you've swung with every ounce of effort in you, to see a ball travel that far ... it's more than satisfying.

After we switch, and I pitch to Hudson a little, I kick the dirt off my cleats. "All right, man, I have to go study. Have an exam for my Revolutionary War and Early American Establishments course tomorrow."

Hudson rolls his eyes. "Boone, man, you don't need to study. You're going to make millions of dollars as a ballplayer."

I smile and wave as I walk backward, away from him. "And if I don't, I'll have a teaching degree to fall back on."

How do you tell someone that you have to get a degree because your father never had one? How do you explain that by his lack of education, and being laid off at the age of fifty-five, he can't get a job but can't afford to retire? How do you detail the number of professional athletes who actually go pro, and of those who do, how many have a career-ending injury and have nothing to fall back on?

You can't. No one understands this until they're living in it. Until they have to watch their mother work three jobs to support their family. Until they see her physically pick her husband up off the couch for the fifth night in a row because he's too drunk to make it to bed.

That's what I lived with, well, still live with. Except now, I don't have to see it every day. Dad lost his job at the local oil plant halfway through my senior year. Actually, about a month after my breakup with Annabelle. Jesus, what shitty timing.

He'd gotten the job straight out of high school, didn't have anything but his diploma and two nickels to rub together. He'd worked his way up over the years, became a foreman, was a senior guy on the team. All until the plant was bought out and his salary was deemed too high for his position, which believe me, he didn't make nearly as much as he deserved. But, they laid him off, replacing him with some twenty-year-old just like me who would take half the pay.

My father sank into a deep depression, especially after a job search with no college degree at fifty-five left him essentially no options. He began to drink. All. The. Time. There wasn't a day that second half of senior year, or since, that I didn't come home to him halfway drowned in a whiskey bottle.

Thank God that I'd gotten scholarships and that I'd been drafted and would soon sign a deal. Being a student-athlete essentially prevented me from getting any kind of job, and the only reason my family has stayed afloat is because my mom is a fucking warrior. She's kept the lights on and food on the table. And just like always, there was scarce little other money to go around.

But all of that would change now. I would be making money.

I would be able to contribute. And maybe, just maybe, I'd be able to get Dad sober. To shove it in his face that I hadn't given up, like him. And that even if I didn't make it in the major leagues, I would still have a college degree to fall back on.

I would succeed either way.

14

I'm disgusted by myself. For letting Boone kiss me, letting him take over.

He'd always been the strong but silent type. People mistook him for a pushover or not that interesting, when really, there was all of this barely controlled masculinity just under the surface. He might play the shy guy, might let people believe he was just a focused baseball player, but he had an agenda of his own. Always.

I had to push him away after he had completely robbed me of breath or thought. I'd made a horrible mistake. Instead of showing him how much he'd hurt me back, I'd opened myself up too wide. He'd seen the vulnerability and gotten the upper hand. How could I be so stupid?

Sucking a breath in, I mentally go through the mantra I've been chanting to myself since Kenneth Kutch's assistant emailed me with a meeting date two days ago. He'd had something open up in his calendar, and could I come in for the conversation he wanted to have with me?

I couldn't say no, but I thought I would have more time to mentally prepare myself.

The mantra plays over and over in my head. *Cold as ice, cold as ice.*

If I could steel myself to any kind of emotion, especially nerves, I would appear confident and capable.

I have only ever been to the headquarters for the Flipping Channel two times before. Once, when I signed my intern paperwork and took a drug test. And second, to negotiate my contract to actually appear on the show. What I got to stand in front of the camera and provide design advice for Ramona was chump change compared to the dollars this place was shelling out to its stars.

Walking into the boardroom, I make sure to leave my hands by my side, not wipe them on my skirt. Giving off the appearance of one hundred percent confidence often gives me one hundred percent confidence. I practically invented faking it until you make it.

Kenneth Kutch sits at the head of the white-washed farmhouse conference table. The room is done in a modern classic design, with traditional Texas wood decor mixed with modern light fixtures and geometric vases lining every surface.

Kenneth is the power and influence behind the Flipping Channel. He started with two TV shows in the eighties and a bunch of filler content from the Home and Garden Channel which had been around for much longer. And slowly, he's built the home of Ramona and James' show into one of the most watched channels on TV.

He has money, a cast of contracting and design stars, a wife thirty years younger than him and a penchant for surprising the hell out of the network with whatever idea came to his mind next.

And hopefully, his next idea has something to do with me.

"Ms. Mills, thank you for coming in." He stands, shaking my hand.

I nod. "Thank you for asking me to come in."

The less I say, the better. Let him think I am doing him a favor. If you act like the boss, others will see it, subconsciously, and respect you.

He motions for me to sit and launches right into it.

"Are you happy on the show?"

I'm a little surprised he asks that, that he wants to know. "Yes, I am. It's a huge accomplishment for me to be on such a successful show at my age. I learn a lot from James and Ramona, and I love what we do. Obviously, interior design is my passion. I'm very happy on the show."

Kenneth nods slowly, eyeing me like a panther circling its prey. I shiver slightly, and I hope he doesn't see it. Something is off.

"So, you would be opposed to going in a different direction ..." It's a question and statement.

I falter. "I ... I'm not sure I follow."

"Right now, you're on that wholesome show with James and Ramona. That is their market, they're pulling in the families and the married couples and conservatives. But when we saw you, we knew how big of a star you'd be."

I shift uncomfortably ... something in the air doesn't feel right. I can't put my finger on it, but my hackles are rising.

He folds his hands on the conference table. "We want to make a big splash on the network. Hit the audience with a fresh, sarcastic, sexy show. Wham! We want Annabelle Mills to be in your face, with all of her beauty and decor ideas. Think of it as Texas beauty queen meets demolition princess meets *Girls Gone Wild*."

What. The. Fuck. When they approached me about this meeting, I had no idea it would be about having my own show. Nor did I think, when I eventually landed my own show, that I'd have to be a mix of Playboy Bunny and Martha Stewart. I am so not okay with this.

I wish I'd hired an agent or a lawyer to help me with this instead of assuming I could handle absolutely anything. My dad had suggested when I'd signed my first contract for appearing on James and Ramona's show, that I should get someone to represent me, but I dismissed his worries as foolish. My freaking ego just hadn't allowed me to admit I needed guidance through this.

"You want me to take my clothes off?" I deadpan.

I should get up and walk out of here, but I stay in the seat.

"No, no! That's not what we're saying at all. Just a little leg here, some well-placed shots. The show would be about your design expertise, do not get me wrong. We are very interested in your eye for interiors. But the network needs new blood. And we think you could liven it up. We're prepared to offer you a very enticing deal in return for two seasons of the show, with an option for the third. Think of how much exposure this could bring you."

Exposure.

The most important thing to make my mother sit up and take notice. I'd be headlining a show, one that would hopefully garner a lot of attention.

"I'm open to entertaining it. Can I see something in writing?" I counter him because I'm not stupid.

He chuckles. "Smart girl. We'll have something drawn up. The whole process of contract negotiation, branding, show direction ... it'll be months before we even start shooting. But, I think this could be a huge hit. We'll be in touch."

He was dismissing me, and I took the hint. I rose, thanking him and starting for the conference room door.

"And, Annabelle?" I turn at his voice. "Don't mention this conversation to James and Ramona."

That can't be anything good.

15

BOONE

Hudson hands me a shot, and I wave him off.

I can almost taste the slick burn of it sliding down my throat.

It's been a rough week. I had three midterms, God, I couldn't believe it was actually almost March and I'd been here for going on three months. And we'd had a special trainer in from Florida, one who works at the spring training facility for the big Texas team, and he almost killed our team. He had us running, squatting, jumping, throwing and hitting until we practically threw up. This guy was of the mind that baseball players needed to be just as in shape as athletes that ran around fields nonstop for three hours.

My body hurt, my mind hurt, and I wanted to drown it all away in alcohol so badly. But my past held me back. Becoming my father held me back.

Instead, I head out to the dance floor when he tells me to follow him, thinking tonight might be a good opportunity to burn off some stress with sex. I haven't had it in a while, and my right hand was getting awfully familiar. My cock tingles at the idea of sinking into something warm and tight.

Yes, that is just the kind of relief I need.

I find a willing partner rather quickly, a blonde so short that her ass barely reaches my hips even though she's wearing spiky heels. I take hold of her waist, backing her up into me, and let myself feel the beat of the song. Her hands begin to explore behind her back, up and down my thighs, over my zipper as we grind, and up until they lace around my neck.

My dick hardens on natural instinct, having not been given attention from a female in a good minute. I caress her smooth skin, get lost in the moment and the music. There is nothing like being in a dark, crowded, loud place to make your inhibitions suspend for a little while.

"Whoops." A cold splash of something runs down my right pant leg.

I jump, startled from the wetness and thrown off because of what I was just imagining doing to this nameless stranger.

I look to my right, and there is Annabelle with an evil grin dancing on her lips.

"Oh my God! I'm soaked!" The blonde cries out over the boom of the music. "What the fuck did you do that for?"

She's glaring at Annabelle, who has the fakest look of innocence on her face I've ever seen. Besides that, she looks fucking edible. Christ, I'm mad that I'm hard right now because my balls tighten, and I have to suck in a breath from the electric shock that moves down my spine just looking at her. She's wearing a dress so short that it might as well be a shirt, with a neckline that rises high onto her slim column of neck. I know that if she turns around, the dress will scoop so low in the back that it will give away almost everything. I just have a feeling. Her hair is piled on top of her head in a tumble of curls, and she looks like sex on heels.

I've always secretly loved that she's almost the same height as me in those teetering, spiked shoes. Almost like she's a formidable opponent to my tall height.

"It was an accident, I swear." Her devilish smirk says it was anything but.

The blonde looks up at me in disgust. Does she think I was in on this or something?

"You really are the fucking devil." I glower at Annabelle.

My dance partner runs off in search of a paper towel and her friends, and we're left in a stare down on the dance floor.

Annabelle sways from her buzz and the beat. "In the flesh, baby."

"What the fuck is wrong with you? Can't you see that I don't want to be around you! Just leave me alone." My blood pressure is climbing, and I'm furious.

She's always fucking with my head. Always causing shit and then acting like she hasn't done a thing.

"That's fine, go dance on sluts all night. What do I care?"

Clearly, she cares, or she wouldn't have come over here and started yelling at me about it. Always drama with Annabelle. She looks wild, one too many drinks in her, and I'm not in the mood. Something in the air tonight is making me horny and ticked off instead of happy and flirty ... not that I'm ever really happy and flirty. But her being here, cockblocking me even if I didn't actually intend to take that girl home, is casting a dark cloud over the whole night.

"Anna, I think you should calm down." Harper appears beside her.

"Get crazy here out of my face." I shoot Harper a warning, that I am about to snap on Annabelle at any point.

"Crazy? Yeah, that's me. Drama, right? You're so pathetic, Boone Graham." Anna flicks up her middle finger.

"Says the drunk girl yelling at the guy whose heart she broke in a crowded club. Talk about pathetic." I wave her off and begin to walk away.

Right out the doors, past the small line gathered outside, of girls in tight dresses and dudes in button-downs waiting to get inside.

Speed walking around the corner, I try very hard to take deep breaths in and out of my nose. My hands shake, and I feel dizzy, and I'm the only person in that club that didn't drink a drop of alcohol.

Her voice comes at me as soon as I get around the back to where my car is parked.

"Just walk away, right? That's what your best at!"

The muscles in my back ripple with tension and barely-there restraint. "And being a selfish brat is what you're best at, right?"

She's clacking toward me in those heels, all hellfire and venom. I back up, the quiet, dark back parking lot desolate aside from our pissing match. "Why did you kiss me the other night?"

"You started it!" I throw my hands up.

Annabelle scoffs. "And then radio silence. Takes what he wants and slinks away, ghosting me."

It's almost as if she's talking to herself, but the words bruise my heart. How could we have hurt each other so badly in such a short amount of time all those years ago?

"What is it that you want from me, Annabelle? You want attention?" I practically roar, so pissed off at this point that I might haul off and punch the brick building beside us.

"Well, you never gave it to me before, so who knows what that even feels like?" Annabelle still has that smug grin on her face.

"Will you just shut the fuck up?"

My patience, what's left of it, snaps. I'm so annoyed and turned-on and furious and head over heels crazy when it comes to this girl that I can't even see straight.

I push her up against the building, the brick cutting into my right palm and probably into her back. My left hand grips her chin roughly and I'm a goner, pushing my tongue into her mouth even as I swallow her protest. I'm pretty sure Annabelle slaps me on the arm, hard enough to make a smacking sound echo off the pavement, but she's scaling me, wrapping her legs around my waist, so I don't stop.

"I hate you," I hiss as my lips latch onto her neck, laying fire to her skin as I press her into the wall.

"I hate me, too." Her sentence barely registers before she pulls my shirt up and over my head, leaving me bare-chested.

My hands are under her dress, seeking her heat. When I find her lacy underwear, I push them aside with two fingers and sink them deep into her.

"Oh, God!" Annabelle cries, fully hanging on me now as I fuck her with my hand.

Adrenaline and lust are going off like bombs inside me, my heart rate gallops like a racehorse about to have an embolism. I can't suck in enough air. I'm surrounded by her, and while I feel like I'm drowning, I also feel like I'm living for the first time in years.

"If you don't get in my car right now, I'm going to fuck you right here in public," I growl, my fingers still stroking inside her.

She makes an unintelligible noise, unwinding her legs from where I hold them at my waist. I pause to gaze at her for just a second.

Mussed hair, sex-bitten lips, the neck of her dress askew. Wild eyes, drunk limbs, lust personified.

There is no evil this woman could do to make me not want her. She's cheated on me, taunted me, been hateful and cold. And still, I know where this will end. With my cock buried deep inside of her in my back seat.

Annabelle Mills is my biggest weakness, and I'm giving up trying to stop myself from giving in.

I grab her hand and pull her with me, struggling to wrench my keys free from my pocket because of the tent my dick has created in my jeans.

When I finally unlock it, I command her,

"Take your underwear off and get in the car."

16

I t's always the quiet ones.

I knew it would be this way. I've been with other guys before. Boastful guys, egotistical ones who were more like show ponies in the sack than actual thoroughbreds. I would try to get out of my own head, to take the lead and be the ice queen and take my pleasure. Because they certainly weren't focused on what felt good for me.

But sex with Boone? God damn, it's *always* the quiet ones.

All of that repressed sexuality and quiet demeanor ... he lets it all go when he's about to connect us in the back seat of his car.

"You just couldn't leave it alone, Annabelle. And now, I have to know. You let another man have you first, but I promise, you'll remember what's about to happen here every single time you touch yourself. Every single time another man touches you. You'll want me. This. I'll be the one in your head and on your skin every time you think about fucking."

Boone is hovering over me, his words rolling off his tongue like orgasm-loaded dynamite. I'm panting, writhing as I lie beneath him in the back seat of his SUV. We're bent at difficult angles, my dress pushed up and his jeans and boxers around his ankles. It's an inferno in here, and the air is stilted and steamy.

But all I can think about is him. How much I want him, how I've waited so long for this moment. *I'm finally having sex with Boone Graham.*

I know though, as he rolls on a condom, that I can't let him have the last word. I have to also protect myself from the emotions in this. I won't fall, I can't. This is it. We're going to have this night, and that will be it. It has to be.

"Just get on with it then. Show me this magic dick of yours that you won't shut the fuck up about," I taunt him, having to be the brat he accuses me of being.

Boone's caramel eyes flash in the light of the dashboard, and I brace myself as he starts to enter me.

So deliciously full.

The thought absorbs into my brain as Boone lets out a long, slow sigh, his chin dropping to his chest as we both watch him disappear inside of me in the dark light of the car.

At the same time that he is completely sheathed in me, our eyes flicker up to gaze at one another. How long have we both waited for this? Why does it feel like the world is ruled by madness and hedonism?

Boone begins to move, and I have to raise one hand above my head to keep him from knocking my skull through the car door. Not that I'd care much in this moment, what he's doing to me feels too damn good.

My other hand fists in his shirt, grasping him, trying to hold him close. Trying to remember every minute detail of this tiny moment of love, the only one we'll ever get. If this is the only capacity in which I'll experience Boone wanting me, just one last time, I'll take it even if it breaks me.

He stares at me, eyes stormy and greedy, taking more and

more from me as we moan and grunt. Is he thinking the same thing?

Too quickly, I'm falling over the edge, my body going from a tightly pulled knot to a million pieces as Boone skillfully manipulates my orgasm on and on and on until I feel like I can't breathe.

On the tail end of my climax, I feel his muscles bristle one at a time. Tensing and then going lax, and he bends down.

"I always knew it would be like this." His whisper curls into my ear as he comes, those eyes pinned to mine.

It's the most raw, masculine thing I've ever had the honor of watching. Seeing the expression on Boone's face as he comes apart is something I will never scrub from my memory. It's the image I'll think about after this when I'm lying in bed alone.

I stare up at the ceiling of his car, the alcohol and orgasm seeping out of my limbs, as Boone pants lightly in my ear. The weight of him is delicious, it's welcoming, and I realize it's been a long time since I've felt comfortable in another person's arms.

But just as I'm about to wrap my hands around the back of his neck, to silently nuzzle into him for just a little longer, he moves off of me. He sits up, disposes of the condom into a tissue he grabs out of the front seat, zips his jeans back up, and opens the car door.

I guess that's the end of it, then.

My knees are shaking as I follow him out, and there is a pit in my stomach that has waves of nausea dancing up and down my spine. I lie to myself, pretend it's the aftereffects of the alcohol, when really I know that it's anxiety about what happens next.

There is a second of awkwardness, with neither of us looking at each other or saying anything.

"Good night." Boone's voice caresses my skin, and I have to bite back a sigh remembering what we just did.

Was he going to leave me here in this dark parking lot, alone?

No, Boone wasn't that guy. He'd driven me home from the ballpark even though that had been awkward as hell. But right now, he's not offering to drive me home.

My brain is fuzzy from sex, so it takes a moment to click. He's not going to offer. He wants me to walk back to the front of the club, so he can rest assure he didn't leave me here in this parking lot. But … he's not going to make sure I get home.

Crashing against my ribcage and subsequently breaking, my heart sinks as if it were a drowning thing falling leagues into the sea. What the hell was I doing? Somewhere between telling myself this would be the only time and the moment Boone whispered in my ear, a spark of hope had lit me up. I'd thought this was him forgiving me.

But he'd only been answering a question that he'd long waited for an answer to. And now that he had it, he was done with me.

I turn, understanding my marching orders, and try not to let a single tear fall by way of freezing my heart once more.

It didn't work.

17

Campus is bustling at noon on a Wednesday as I come out of my Standardized Tests and Teaching Outside the Box course.

March has arrived and so has spring in Texas. Which is pretty much like summer anywhere else, but people from here think they need a sweater when temps reach a brisk seventy-four.

I don't mind the weather change. It means baseball season is coming. We're about to have our first spring training game, and I am more than ready to get out on the field and show this team what I can do. Hopefully, I can graduate, earn my stripes and then hopefully be promoted to the big time.

My phone begins to buzz in my pocket, and I pick it up as I head for the science and engineering building where my next class is. I may be getting a teaching degree specified in history, but they still make you take all of the subjects. Science included. Which I'm shit at.

"Hey, Mama." I pick up, smiling.

Mom has always been my biggest supporter. Even when Dad was functioning and sober and working, she'd still been the one who was always at my games. The one who talked about the big dream, who never once tinged it with doubt by suggesting that only one in however many amateur athletes actually made it to the pros.

"Buddy, how is everything? I miss you." She sounds tired.

She was always tired these days. I try not to ball my fist at my side in anger about Dad and resolve myself to think about the money I'd be giving her any day now.

"Everything is good. Studying, sleeping and training, you know the drill." I don't like to worry her.

The clang of pots could be heard in the background. "And how is the team? Do you like the coaches? Same caliber equipment as Pennsylvania?"

Mom is a baseball mama through and through. Had invested every bit of herself into the sport since the day I started playing.

"Even better than Carolina, Mama. The team is good, it's a faster pace, challenging, but in a good way. I'm excited for you to come down for a game once the season starts. I miss you, too."

"I'll see if I can take a day or two off. You know I'm so proud of you, I can't wait to watch you be a star on that field. Well, you've always been a star."

I sigh. "Mom, once I negotiate my contract in the next couple of weeks, you can quit working three jobs. Not that you should have to anyway."

She makes a *pshh* sound. "You know I don't care about that money. That's your money."

I put an end to her polite dismissal of the money immediately. "Mama, I'm not taking no for an answer. You deserve this money, you've put just as much sweat and tears into this as I have. And I don't want to see you working this hard. He should be working, he should get his lazy ass up off that couch!"

My blood is simmering, threatening to boil over.

"Oh, buddy, don't talk like that. You're dad has had a hard time—"

And now I'm flaming mad. "Mom, stop doing that!" I don't want to yell at her, but I'd had enough of this. "He's the man of the family. And I'm not saying that women can't be the bread-winners, but he's not even helping contribute. He's a lazy, drunk piece of shit."

"Boone Martin Graham, I didn't raise you to curse, and I did not raise you to talk about your father that way." Her voice is harsh.

I sigh. "Sorry, ma'am."

She clears her throat and brushes over the topic like she didn't just snap at me. "All right, buddy, you keep working hard, and let me know your schedule when we get closer to April. I love you so much."

"Love you, too, Mama." We hang up and I stare at my phone for a second.

The hate for my father, for our position in the world, for everything that has worked against me up until this point ... it all bubbles up in my veins. That hate keeps me hungry, pushes me forward.

The phone call is exhausting, so it takes me a minute to register the scene in front of me as I come to stand at the bottom of the stairs leading to the entrance of the science building.

"Oh my God, are you okay?"

"Are you hurt?"

People crowd around someone lying on the stairs, and I hear tiny gasps of pain from the person lying in the middle of the circle.

As bodies move and shuffle, I see a familiar face, tight and pinched in agony, lying on the ground.

Annabelle.

I move before I think her name, my body reacting to the

instinct to heal her pain rather than do what is better for me, probably, and just walk the other way. I push past the people just acting like idiots and staring down at her.

My heartbeat thumps in my ears, and I can't get to her fast enough.

We haven't talked since I pulled out of her in my car and she slowly walked away as we looked at each other. And the last time we were on a set of stairs like these together, I was telling her it was over.

But now, I don't even hesitate. I move into the middle of the crowd, bend down, and scoop her up. Without even thinking, I pull her to my chest, looping my arms under her knees and supporting her shoulders.

"Ah, what?" Those chocolate brown eyes hold pain and confusion.

"What hurts?" I ask as I walk away from the people on the steps, carrying her.

"My hand, maybe my wrist. I missed a step, these heels, I'm so embarrassed ..." She hides her face behind her good hand.

Looking at her shoes, way too high to be wearing on a school day, and then down at her left hand, I can already tell that there is probably a break somewhere. Just an athlete's eye, I've seen guys pop shoulders out and break ankles more than anyone on this campus.

She needs a doctor, and not the shitty campus ones. I want to take her to my trainers at the Triple AAA facility, but I don't think I'm actually allowed to do that. So, emergency room it is. The hospital in Austin is held in high regard and I know she'll be treated quickly there ... or so I hope. Maybe we can both throw around some local celebrity to have her seen sooner.

"Boone?" Her eyes hold pain and questions.

"Don't worry, I've got you," I tell her as I load her into my truck. "I've got you."

"So, who did you punch?"

Cain and Harper walk in hand in hand, and the pain medication they gave me has me a little happier than my normal personality. I can feel it, but there isn't anything I can do to keep my thoughts inside.

"You guys are grossly happy. It's kind of cute. Also, I punched no one. My hot heels made me trip." I smile.

Cain rears back and stares at me, ribbing Harper. "Did she just smile?"

Harper chuckles. "Got you on some good stuff there, huh?"

I grin, pointing at her. "Sister, they definitely do."

My hand still has a heartbeat, but I could no longer remember the pain of them setting my wrist bones back into place. The drugs are a nice bonus, but the cast they put me in is garish and cumbersome. I will not be able to film the show with this eyesore.

"So you tripped? Did you drive yourself here?" Cain looks a little concerned.

I shake my head vehemently. "A knight in shining armor picked me up, took me in his chariot!"

Again, Harper laughs at me. I laugh too, because this whole situation is just ridiculous. How in the hell had Boone been there at the exact moment I'd fallen down the science building stairs?

"A knight, huh? Did he slay the dragon, too?" Cain begins to tap on the hospital bed I'm lying in. "And how did you get this fancy room for a simple broken wrist? Did you drop my name?"

"No, she dropped mine." Boone stands in the doorway, looking as handsome as Lancelot himself.

"And I might have slayed his dragon." I giggle.

Harper lets out a sharp gasp and then covers her mouth as I cackle. "Oh my God!"

"Damnit, I thought I was the hottest athlete in this town. Can you move back to bumfuck Pennsylvania?" Cain pouts.

Boone walks in, looks down at me, almost checking in. I stare up at him dreamily ... I can't help it. The drugs have taken away all of the self-censorship from my brain to my mouth.

"Some of us are getting paid to be here, Kent." Boone can't resist getting a dig in at his former nemesis.

Cain looks wounded, if not dramatically. "Ganging up on the student-athlete. I see how it is, Graham."

"Hey, I put my years in." The man who picked me up off the stairs on campus turns to me. "How are you feeling?"

"Just dandy, knight." I grin at him.

Inside of my head, I know this is embarrassing. It's embarrassing to be ogling him, to call him my savior, to smile like a moron when he walks into the room. But the drugs rule all and I can't help it.

"She broke her wrist falling down a set of stairs on campus. I got her the private room by signing an autograph for a nurse's son, but don't let that slip. Didn't want her sitting down in the ER while they set the bones. Doctor said it needs to be in a cast for six weeks, and then an ace bandage and physical therapy for four weeks after that. They gave her a prescription for Percocet, but I'd have her stick to Tylenol if she can manage with the pain. Other than that, she's ready to get discharged. Just needs a ride home."

Boone rattles off the doctor's orders as if he'd taken detailed notes, and I actually clap after he's done. But he said I needed a ride home ...

"You're not going to take me home?" I pout.

I might be semi-high, okay fine, I'm really high, but I don't miss the look that Harper and Cain exchange.

Harper nods at Boone, though. "We'll take her to our place. Cain is leaving for a road game anyway, so she can stay with me for a day or two."

I'm still focused on why Boone is leaving me in the first place. "But ... you brought me here."

He walks over to the bed, bending down so close so that I can smell his musk. He presses his lip to my temple, not in a kiss, but just resting them there.

"Feel better, Anna."

I toss and turn as my eyes open, the pain in my wrist radiating up my arm and even causing laser sharp pings to pound against my temple.

"Ugh," I moan in agony.

Harper is there in a flash. "Here, pain pills. And here is some water."

My stepsister holds out the glass and the pills, helping to feed them to me as I press on the bed to sit up with my good hand. She's been a damn saint for the past two days, taking care of me and distracting me while the pain of my broken bones rage within me. And I have to admit, it's been kind of fun having a mom-type figure take care of me while I'm sick and hurting. My dad had always been around to do it, and had been a comforting person in my life, but ... it was different having a mom be there like that. And I almost don't remember anymore the time my mom was in my life like that.

"Thanks." I cough, willing the pain pills to start.

She's withheld the good stuff, instead demanding that I stick to over-the-counter pain remedies. While I know the hospital-grade medication would work wonders, I know she's right. That stuff can be dangerous, and I hate having a fuzzy head. When it comes to alcohol, I don't mind. That wears off quick enough, but the drugs scare me. Addiction scares me even more ... always has for some weird reason.

Harper sits down, setting a plate of cookies on the bed. "I baked while you slept. Figured we could both use some sugar. And you're going to want it, because it's time to spill."

I pick up a warm, gooey chocolate chip cookie and breath in its scent. "Mmm, spill what?"

"What is going on with you and Boone?"

I try to avoid her gaze, but she hits my good arm. "Hey! I kind of need that, or I'll practically be paralyzed."

"So then out with it before I have to maim you permanently. This is sister code, or didn't you know? You have to tell me every-thing that goes on in your love life."

I stink-eye her. "I don't want to know anything going on in your love life. Actually, I'd rather you never even mention Cain and love in the same sentence to me."

"Too bad. Plus, you're the one who convinced me to give him another chance, so that shit is on you. Now out with it."

I sigh, picking up a second cookie. "We kissed a while back."

Harper lets out a gasp through a big bite of cookie. "What!"

But before she can press me for more information, I just

come out with it all. "And then we had sex in his car that night at the club that I spilled a drink on that slut he was dancing with."

Now she just about chokes on said cookie. "I'm sorry, what?"

I blink at her. "I fucked Boone in the back seat—"

"No, nope I got that part, thanks. I just mean ... what in the ever loving hell? I thought you two hated each other. I ... no offense, I thought he hated you."

"Well, thanks, sis. Makes me feel *a lot* better." I roll my eyes.

"Sorry! I just mean ... what are you two? Have you talked about any of this? And why was he the one who brought you to the hospital?"

I shrug, kind of needing to vent about this. Usually, I would keep this balled up inside and let it fester until I became more of a raging asshole than I already am.

"Well, the hospital was a fluke. He just happened to be there when I fell down the stairs. Scooped me right up and put me in his car to take me to the hospital. And then stayed with me and held my hand while they set my wrist."

"And kissed you on the forehead before he left," she adds.

"Yeah ... that too. I have no idea, to be honest, what we are. Or what we're doing. We talked a little bit about it, more like vented at each other about each other. He basically hates me, and I am not proud of what I did, but we've talked about why I did it. I'm not pleased with him either ... he didn't treat me like he should have."

Harper gives me an anxious glance. "I know he didn't. But at the risk of you scratching my eyes out with your cat claws ... have you ever apologized for what you did to him? I know that there were issues before you cheated ... but, you cheated. That is damaging, Anna."

I look down at Harper and Cain's navy blue bedspread. "I'm not sure I was ever really sincere about it."

"Maybe you should start there. Because I think you want a second chance ... am I right?"

I think about the night in the ballpark, and then the night in his car. I would be a liar, liar pants on fire if I didn't admit that I want another chance at something with Boone. He's the only man I have ever felt a spark with, the only one who can coax me out of this ice castle I've built inside of myself.

"Yeah, I think maybe you are."

Harper smiles knowingly, as if she feels bad for me but also holds hope.

"But for now, I think another cookie will be the best remedy. For broken wrists and healing hearts."

19

ANNABELLE

We've been going on filming for six hours now, and my head is throbbing almost as much as my wrist.

"Darlin', you're hurting. If you need to go home—" James attempts to rub my back in a fatherly gesture.

"I don't quit on a shoot, but thanks." I give James a pointed glare.

"All I'm saying is, no one would blame you." He walks away, shaking his head.

He and Ramona have been circling me like protective mama bears all day. Not to mention the owners of this house are making it particularly difficult to make any progress on the design or construction. It's a 1950s ranch-style four bedroom that hasn't seen an upgrade since it was built, probably. Vinyl flooring, an outdated heating and air-conditioning system, and tile kitchen countertops so disgusting that I would use my casted hand to take a sledgehammer to them.

But all the while, these people keep screaming at Ramona about budget. I never enjoy couples like these. The ones who think it'll be easy-peasy to buy a house and renovate, and who love *Hart & Home,* so they just sign up without actually understanding the process, time and money that is involved. Ramona and James are not just going to pay for your renovation, but you'd be surprised at how many people think that.

Guiltily, I think about the contract that was delivered to my house two days ago. I'm typically the total opposite of a procrastinator, but I just can't bring myself to open the big, sealed envelope. Does that mean my icicle of a heart is thawing?

"And you know, you all did not tell us that the floors were going to cost this much! And another thing—"

I cannot listen to these hillbilly morons go on for one more second. Marching up to them, cameras rolling and all, I put a hand on Ramona's shoulder.

"Shut it, Bobbi-Jo. Just shut it. These people are doing spectacular work for you and for a house that you decided on. You made the decision to come on this show, to spend the money, to have industry professionals suggest the best kind of renovation materials and designs. You don't know all of the time and labor that is spent on these projects, nor do you seem to care or appreciate it. So just stop nagging at Ramona and James and let them do their jobs. Trust me, you'll be singing their praises when you're sitting on your one-of-a-kind suede couch eating beef jerky with curlers in your hair!"

Stomping off after my tirade, not bothering to let the moronic clients get a word in, I press my good hand to my chest and rub hard. The frustration I feel, at those clients, at my injury, at the world right now, is threatening to bubble up to the surface. I can't afford, and would never let, a breakdown like the one looming happen on set.

Behind me, I can hear Ramona apologizing and saying something about passionate interns. I don't mind that she plays my little outburst off. We've done this countless times, and I don't mind being the scape-bitch. I was kind of like the scape-goat, but I was put in an evil light.

"Hey, hey, are you okay?" Someone grabs my elbow as I try to brush past them.

I yank it away, looking up, and am stunned to see Boone.

Boone Graham, here. On my turf.

"What're you doing here?" I say softly, my entire mood shifting.

"James said I could come down to set anytime I liked, and I wanted to come thank you for the pie." God, he looks good in his white long sleeve, jeans and workman's boots.

Like he could be my own private handyman.

"Oh, that? It was nothing." I think I might be blushing, and I curse myself. Turn your devil on, girl.

Boone smiles an actual, genuine smile at me. "It was delicious, is what it was."

I wanted to thank him for helping me the day I broke my wrist, and for taking such good care of me until Harper and Cain got to the hospital. So, I'd summoned the inner-pageant queen in me and baked a good ole southern pecan pie and dropped it on his doorstep. I may have had to pull a few strings behind the scenes of the show to get his address, and I felt like a stalker creeping up to his apartment door and stealthily leaving a bakery box there, but clearly it had been appreciated.

"I just wanted to thank you." My eyes cast down, because I suddenly feel shy.

So much has happened between us, and that's just in the last two or three months. I am no longer angry about how we'd broken up, but I was semi-shattered about him leaving me after what happened in his car and then never calling.

"Well, don't mention it." It's clear he's trying his hardest to be nice. "I'm going to say hi to James and get out of here. Don't want to get in the way, you're clearly busy."

I look back at Ramona. "Oh, that? Just high-maintenance clients."

A beat of silence passes. "You're really good at what you do, Annabelle. I've ... caught a couple of episodes when sports isn't on."

That makes me laugh. "Thanks, I think. Glad I can be your non-athletic entertainment."

It's the first non-confrontational conversation we've had in over four years. And at the risk of ruining it, I know I need to follow Harper's advice.

"Listen, Boone ... I just want to say that I'm sorry. I know that I hurt you, I know that I made a huge mistake and that I cost us both a lot of heartache. I just need you to know how truly sorry I am. It might not make it better, but from the bottom of my heart, holding my guilty hands up in surrender, I am sorry."

Those large, caramel eyes blink at me, searching my face for something. I take a shaky breath, because that was a lot for me to admit to, and the apology has been lodged in my chest for far too long.

"I didn't think I'd ever get that from you. I know it probably wasn't easy. Thank you."

I nod, unsure of what to do now. My body, all aquiver within from the sight of him standing there in front of me, wanting him to envelop it. The pull between us is magnetic, and I have to actively fight stepping into him. Especially after the night in the car.

And I was about to do something even crazier than either of us imagined I could. Because I was typically the hard-to-get girl. I didn't ask boys out or even chase them. I was the frigid bitch they needed to win over.

But when it comes to Boone, I found that all of that went out the window.

"Do you think ... could we maybe get dinner sometime?"

I don't go into detail. Maybe he thinks I mean as friends. Maybe he thinks I mean as more. Maybe he can never get to a point of forgiveness to even share a bread basket with me. I hold my casted arm behind my back and cross my pointer and middle finger on my good hand.

Threading a large hand through his hair, Boone smirks at me. "Yeah, yeah I think we could do that."

20

BOONE

I have managed to escape her orbit for years.

I've been clean and sober, I don't shake every time I come within fifty feet of her. I only think about her in those dark, quiet times when I can't help it.

But the minute I stepped foot back in Texas, my addiction was back. I can't stay away from her, even though I hate her. Even though I know she wrecks me every time I get a taste.

Should I give in? Can I change her? Can I control this ... need if we decide to see where this can go? Can I ever truly forgive her for what she did to me?

Is it against everything I've sworn up and down for years if that answer is yes?

Right now, I am too fucking cold to think about all of that. I step out of the cryotherapy chamber, my nuts so shriveled that I am scared to look down for the fear that they may have fallen off. My toes are numb and frozen, the rest of my body shaking with the ice that had just clung to it.

This kind of deep freeze treatment is a bitch while you are in it, but afterward, it feels amazing. And it gives me quicker recovery rates after practices and games. I'm serious, people think I am a crackpot when I say that, but it really does work.

"Man, now I can't chicken out because you did it. And now you saw me. So now I have to go freeze my balls off."

Cain walks into the room where the three cryo chambers stand, opposite from the wall of white leather couches I'm now huddled on wrapped in a fur-lined blanket.

"Have you tried it yet?" I shiver, eyeing the guy who used to be enemy number one in my book.

"Nah, I'm a little chickenshit."

"Trust me, man, it'll do wonders for your rebound rate. You'll come off a game and be able to go right into another a day later."

Cain rolls his shoulders a couple of times. "In that case, balls, meet ice."

I chuckle as he eyes the chamber up and down. "Just do it, man. It's best to jump in the deep end."

He nods, sprints in, and strips off his boxers when the door closes. "Holy fuck, this is like fucking death. I can't make it three minutes."

I shiver just looking at him. "Yeah, you can, dude. Just distract yourself."

Cain nods. "So, what's going on with you and Annabelle?"

I can feel the stern look that comes over my expression. "Do you want to get punched in the face again?"

"Come on, dude, I'm so wifed up it's not even funny. And Annabelle is practically my sister-in-law, as fucked-up as that is. You said distract myself, so I want to know what your intentions are."

My knuckles crack. "Really? This is how you want to distract yourself? Gossip? I thought you were better than that. And why the hell do you think I'd talk to you about this?"

The guy slaps the side of the chamber, as if that'll stop the icy air from sinking it's fingers into his skin. "Yep, this is how I want to distract myself. Now you have two minutes and thirty seconds to lay out your love troubles."

I sigh. "Dude, really?"

He flips me off. "Yes. You act like you have another person to vent this out to."

"I certainly have one who hasn't slept with the girl in question. While she was my fucking girl, I might add."

He rolls his eyes. "Man, seriously, it's all in the past. You need to just forgive her for that and move on, because anyone within a fifty mile radius of you two can see you want to fuck like bunnies."

I still can't wrap my mind around how he, Harper and Annabelle are just so casual about this. This guy, and his cockiness, still pisses me off. He's a superstar, one of those shiny athletes who uses his smile and interview personality just as much as his talent. Sure, he's a hell of a quarterback, but our game and play style are completely different. I'm the strong, keep-my-nose-to-the-grindstone type who lets my work speak for itself. He's a boaster, one of those guys who thinks he's a god.

And how they can all just hang out together is beyond me. It seems, to my injured heart, that I'm the only one truly affected by it.

"How can all of you just be so cool with this?" It boggles my mind.

The clock on the chamber is now down to a minute left. "Look, dude, it took a while. With Annabelle and I, it honestly wasn't personal. We didn't really like each other, and I regret sleeping with her. Even before I met Harper, I regretted that. We went through some shit as friends, but then I met my girl. And damn, at the sake of sounding like a whipped pussy, I am head over heels in love with her. And her mom is married to Annabelle's dad. Believe me, those two girls hated each other at first. We both know Annabelle does not like hot new girls stepping into her territory, and although Harper can be a quiet one, she is *not* one to back down. But now they're family, and that shit runs deeper than petty feuds. Annabelle is actually the one who convinced Harper to give me a second shot when I fucked-up. So yeah, it took a while, but love and family are worth more than bullshit."

The beeper on Cain's chamber buzzes and he grabs his boxers, dances into them, and then scurries out, grabbing a blanket and jumping up and down to keep his legs from going dead with the shock of warm air on them suddenly.

I'm finally regulated back to normal temperatures, and I lean forward, setting my elbows on my knees. "So you're saying I should give her a second chance, even though she fucked-up."

"Hm, you're not as dumb as you look." He chuckles, still hopping back and forth from foot to foot.

I walk past him, clapping a big hand on his shoulder. "Watch it, Kent. I could still knock you clean out. But ... thanks for the advice."

My trip to the cryotherapy chamber took an unexpected turn. It might have frozen each and every one of my blood cells, but it seems to have thawed one muscle in particular. One that has been falling rapidly back under Annabelle's spell.

"I'm so happy it's warm enough for espadrilles again. They're like, the perfect footwear. They look sexy with all of the straps and open toes, but the cork and level bottom make it not even feel like you're wearing heels at all."

Thea struts happily along beside me, our matching smoothie cups in one hand and designer purses in the other.

"It was only cold for all of three months. And don't you know that wedges are out. The Queen says so." I roll my eyes.

"Just because Meghan and Kate aren't allowed to wear them doesn't mean I'm not. I'm a Texas princess and will dress to my honky-tonk's delight, Daisy Dukes and all."

This is why I love her. "You're impossible. But yes, I'm glad it's warm. I don't know why anybody likes sweater weather. Give me maxi dresses and rompers any day."

We stroll along campus, weaving in and out of fellow students as the sun shines over my bare shoulders. Finding a table outside in the quad, we set our stuff down wordlessly and take out our laptops. The purpose of our get together is a study session. There is a huge exam coming up in our Design of the Early Twentieth Century course, and I don't intend on failing.

School has never come easy to me. Sure, I get good grades, but I don't enjoy learning or sitting in class. I'm not a competent test taker; I literally have to browbeat the information into my head by hours upon hours of studying the material.

"All right, so what notes do you have on the model houses and architecture lecture that I missed because of shooting?" I pull Thea's notebook toward me, my brain slipping into study mode.

For the next hour and a half, we sit at our table under a shady oak tree and quiz each other, talking out each session of the course we've participated in and trying to figure out what surprise essay questions might be featured on the exam.

"Hey, Annabelle."

A gruff voice floats over my right shoulder, and I look up, the sunlight filtering past the figure standing above me. The light around the person makes their face dark, and I have to use the hand not wrapped in a cast for four more damn weeks to get a better look.

My heart jumps when the face comes into focus. "Boone, hi."

He sits down next to me on the concrete bench on my side of the table. "What're you ladies up to?"

Thea is already licking her chops. "Studying for a test. But we could be persuaded to stop."

Even though she's my friend and has no idea that Boone is my ex, the big green monster of jealousy still hops up on my back and starts beating its chest to assert that Boone is mine.

Boone chuckles, and I eye him for flirting with her. "I won't interrupt for long. I'm Boone, by the way."

"Thea." She extends her hand and bats her lashes.

I roll my eyes. "Down, girl. He only has room enough in his life for one drama queen."

She pouts at me, but I can see the interest in her eyes.

Clearly, I'll have a lot of questions fired at me as soon as Boone gets up and leaves this table.

Turning to me, Boone's knee grazes mine and I try to stifle the delicious tingle that shoots down my spine. "I was wondering if you were free for dinner tonight? I know it's last minute, but the season will be starting in three days, and I wanted to get out with you before my life turns into a chaotic mess."

He's asking me to dinner. The inner-teenager inside of me does a wild celebration dance, kind of like it did the first time he asked me out back in Haven. I have to gulp three times before I answer, because I'm scared that when I speak, my heart might just jump out of my throat.

"Yes, I'd love to. I don't have to go to set tonight, so I'm free."

He stands, wrapping his knuckles on the table. "Great. Text me your address, you still have my number, right? I'll pick you up at eight."

Riding in the same car I'd been sprawled out in the back seat of a month ago is fairly strange.

I keep wanting to turn my head around and look at the spot where Boone had been between my wide open legs, but I know that if I do, he'll notice. Not that he isn't thinking the same thing, I keep seeing his eyes flit to the rearview mirror.

"How has your week been?" I ask, trying to start a conversation.

Boone controls the car with one hand propped up on the steering wheel. He commands it, and I imagine that fist wrapped around a very different kind of stick shift. I can't help it that everything this man does reminds me of sex. I only got one taste of it, in this very car, and it wasn't nearly enough.

"Been okay. We have our first game this Sunday, opening day at the ballpark, so it's been pretty hectic. A lot of media, more practice, plus I have to keep up with my schoolwork. At least there is only two months of school left, so after I graduate I can just focus on the season. But, yeah, it's just been an adjustment. How about you? Do you work with Ramona and James every day?"

It feels nice, hearing about his day and him asking about mine. It's ... normal. We never did normal. We had the typical high school relationship. Hang out at the movies or mall in a group, and then just fall into being together. There were no dates, no real, deep conversations. We mostly made out and went to parties together. But there was still that underlying spark that kept us gravitating toward each other, and it was still here now.

"Not every day, but most days. We shoot on Mondays, Tuesdays and Thursdays, but I'll inevitably get called in to a site or their studio at their house to go over some detail probably about two other days a week."

"Isn't that intense with your class schedule? And you're only, what now, twenty-one?"

I nod. "Good guess, yeah, I'm old for my grade, my birthday is in October."

"October seventeenth, right?" He glances over at me and then puts his eyes back on the road.

"Wow, didn't think you remembered my birthday." I am shocked.

Boone just smiles. "So, does the show make you miss class a lot?"

Shrugging, I try to speak through the surprise of Boone remembering a detail about me. "I do, but my advisor helps me butter up the teachers and they all know what great publicity it is for the design program at the college that one of their students is a featured intern on one of the most highly rated home flipping shows on TV."

"That's true. Have you ever thought about just doing the show full time?" He seems genuinely curious.

"I won't lie and say I haven't. But I want to check the box of having a degree."

"You always were a perfectionist. Always had to have everything in its right order." He adjusts his position, and my eyes can't help but stray to the crotch of his black jeans.

I kind of like that he's driving and can't quite fully focus on me. It gives me time to inspect every part of his face and physique.

Swallowing the lump in my throat, I give him a small smile. "Says the guy who has a whopping major league baseball contract but is still in college. What's that about, anyway?"

Boone's eyes slide to me, look at my mouth, and then flit back to the road. "Eh, it's a long, boring story."

His silence tells me we won't be discussing that topic further.

We've been on the road for about twenty minutes, and are somewhere in the suburbs of Austin, when Boone turns the car into a parking lot. Looking up, I see the sign on a building as he maneuvers the car into a spot. It reads, The Alamo.

"Super creative name for a restaurant in Texas." I roll my eyes.

"Don't knock it until you try it. I know, the name is corny, but they serve the best fried pickles here that I've ever eaten."

My heart leaps. "I love fried pickles."

"I know." Boone smiles as we exit the car.

He makes no move to open my door for me, which I kind of prefer. I'm not an invalid, I can open doors and carry bags and I'm just fine with a breakfast smoothie on the go and no tray in my bed. I've always been less romantic than everyone around me, and I'm glad that Boone isn't acting the part of the chivalrous male. Although, I'll take pink peonies any day of the week. Just because I love the smell and they're pretty to look at.

"You remembered that?" I'm kind of in awe.

He stops before opening the restaurant door for me. "Annabelle, despite what you've assumed, I didn't totally have my head stuck up my ass when it came to dating you in high school. I know things about you, probably more than you told me or let on. So just go with it. Commit yourself to the idea that we're going to have a great date."

So, it is a date. I hadn't been sure, but he just confirmed it. And to prove that I am committed, I lace my fingers through his in a sign of accepting that this is going to be a romantically-themed evening. Hand-holding with the guy you are out on the town with isn't cheesy, it's just good karma.

And by good karma, I meant that maybe good luck and a little fate will find its way to the back seat of his car again.

22

BOONE

The afternoon before my first game with the Texas major league affiliate team, I was called into the front offices to sign my contract.

When they set that paperwork down in front of me, and I saw the number of zeros laid out in the contract, my eyes nearly fell out of my head. To have that much money given to me, to know that it was going into my bank account, that my mom and I were going to be okay, that I could support her ...

Only kids who came from nothing would understand what that felt like.

And now here I am, standing on the first base line with my teammates as a third-grade student from an Austin public school sings the National Anthem. My first game as a professional baseball player.

I won't say that I can't believe it, because that would be a lie. From the time I knew that I had a knack for baseball, I believed that I would get here. By working my ass off, listening to coaches, and keeping on the straight and narrow, I made my dream come true.

Annabelle couldn't come to the game today, even though I'd invited her to on our date last night. That's right, two dates in two days. Between the man and woman who formerly hated each other. With each passing second I spend with her, trying to move on and have a fresh start, I realize that I'd forgotten just how much I like Annabelle.

She is witty and has this dry sense of humor that is almost mean but sarcastic at the same time. I don't feel like I have to pamper her or boost her ego, she's confident enough to do that on her own. But, it did feel good to take care of the check knowing that she didn't expect it. It felt good to hold her in my arms and lay my lips down on hers.

Surprisingly, on our two dates, I was able to push past our history and begin a fresh chapter with her. I didn't think about her betrayal every time she spoke, and my blood didn't boil when she made a biting, sarcastic remark.

The anthem finishes, and we applaud, and then high fives and "let's get 'em's" are exchanged.

Sand and grass crunch under my cleats, and I breathe in the faint smell of peanuts, popcorn and cotton candy. A day at the ballpark is better than any place on earth to me.

When I get out to center field, the crowd begins to go wild. Voices rain down on me, and I realize they're coming from the giant screen right above my head.

Looking up at the video board, James and Ramona's faces light up the screen. They start to speak, and the crowd goes wild.

"We just wanted to wish the team good luck, and to say that we love supporting all of the young men who work so hard at the sport of baseball. Go Austin!"

They raise their hands in celebration on the screen, and the crowd goes wild. Turning around, I ready myself for the first pitch, hitting my gloved hand with the other fist.

I never expected what happens next.

There's another cheer from the crowd, and then a familiar voice fills my ears. My back is to the video board, so I whirl back around to see Annabelle's face shining down at me, large and looming above my position on the field.

"And I just want to give a special shout out to outfielder Boone Graham! We're all so happy to have you here in Austin, and we know you'll do great things! Go get 'em, ya'll!"

Catcalls and hollers rise up from the crowd, and I hear someone sitting in the bleacher seats nearby yell, "Get her phone number, buddy!"

My cheeks are surely redder than a pig on a spit, and I have to pull my hat down low to drown out some of the ruckus and focus on the game. She's essentially taken us public and hadn't even consulted me on it. Were we even technically anything? We've only had two dates thus far where we managed not to scratch each other's eyes out, and that did not a relationship make.

Now some stupid local gossip reporter will run this on her Instagram stories, or blog, and essentially start some tabloid nonsense about how we were having a baby and that someone had spotted Annabelle with a bump. That kind of shit always happens, and I had just broken into the echelon where it ran rampant.

Meanwhile, I am still trying to grapple with my feelings of distrust for Anna and resolve them so that we can explore the underlying attraction we still have for each other. But seeing her so vulnerable when she broke her wrist, and taking care of her in the hospital, has shown me just how strong my feelings still are. Even if I tried to bury them deep down inside for so many years.

"Hey man, looks like you have a not so secret admirer. And

she's smokin' hot!" Kincaid, our left fielder, raises his eyebrows at me as he shouts over the crowd.

I wave him off. "Yeah, yeah. Let's just focus on getting this W."

Blocking the noise out, I push the questions of Annabelle and me out of my head and let my game attitude overcome me. It's this place of Zen, of laser-sharp focus that I've perfected over the years. When it's at its best, I don't even hear the crowd. When it's at its best, I can pinpoint the ball whizzing down at me from one hundred feet up in the air.

The first, second and third innings are played with little to no excitement, just clean strikes and a couple ground balls. Our team comes up to bat in the fourth inning, and the rotation has swung around to have me picking up my Louisville Slugger first.

I take the plate, grinding my cleats into the red clay and sizing up the pitcher. So far he's had an accurate targeting of the strike zone, but he's impatient. He doesn't like when batters wait him out, and I know that I'm not going to swing until there is a full count. Wear him down mentally, and then take my chance when he whips a fast ball at me.

It's not arrogant to say that what I predicted ended up being reality. He gets twitchy when I don't budge at the first two pitches, one a strike and one a ball. Because after that, he throws two more balls and I know I've spooked him.

And I take that opportunity to let the crowd in, to take the blinders off for a minute and let their chants and screams become the adrenaline pumping through my veins. Here it is, he thinks this is going to be his ace.

I can already feel it, the tenor of the air, the angle of the ball, before it connects with my bat and I swing for the heavens. The crack resounds through my ears and stings in my muscles. But the burn is *so* good, my body rejoices at the pain. The noise of the cheers and my teammates whoops greet me as I round home plate, stomping on it like it's a new land only I have conquered.

My second at bat in professional baseball, and I hit a homer. If it feels this good in Triple AAA, I can't imagine what it's going to feel like when I make it to The Show.

23

The smell of popcorn and gummy candy fill my nose, and the sound of arcade games rings out as I pay for mine and Annabelle's tickets.

"A movie guy. I never would have pegged you for a movie guy." Annabelle eyes me scrupulously.

"Believe it. I've been wanting to see this movie since the minute I was alerted about the trailer coming out on YouTube." I check our tickets once more, making sure that we have prime seats.

I reserved them online this afternoon, in between class and practice, when Annabelle told me she could probably shrug out of work early and go on a date. Wanting to do something fun, something high school-ish because we'd never done it back then, I decided on taking her to the local movie theater to the see the new superhero movie everyone is buzzing about.

"You're a nerd ... I guess I never realized that until now. You have comic books instead of Playboys under your bed, don't you?" She accuses me as I take her hand, lace my fingers through it, and lead us to the snack line.

"No one has Playboys under their bed anymore. Free porn is

easily accessible on the Internet." This makes Anna chuckle. "But, I may have some graphic novels at my apartment."

"Graphic novels, give me a break. Those are full-on, nerded-out, comic books. Oh, and I want Twizzlers. You're making me sit through this, you owe me candy."

I look down at her, smiling. "You're going to love this movie, I'm telling you. I wish I'd had time to adequately binge the entire comic book universe worth of movies with you, since you'd understand it more, but that's okay. You're still going to love it. Then you're going to beg me to watch all of the individual character movies with you."

We move up as each person or couple in front of us pays for their snack. "I wouldn't count on it, I don't really like movies."

I drop her hand and turn to stare at her like she's just told me she is an alien from Mars. "Uh, what? You don't like movies? I didn't even think that was a thing humans could do."

Anna shrugs. "I just never really got into them. And now I have no time. The last movie I saw in a movie theater was probably when I was about twelve?"

She says all this normally, as if the rest of the people inside this theater are the weird ones for enjoying motion pictures. "I don't even know what to say. I'm floored."

It's our turn to buy snacks, and good thing, because I'm not sure I can talk to Annabelle without getting into an argument with her right here in the line. She always has to have some alternative opinion, or make you feel like you're the one in the wrong.

But as we walk to our designated theater, I take a breath and swallow that emotion. Because I'm fairly confident that she's going to love this movie. And even if she doesn't, she won't be able to get bored when all of those hot guys are on the screen. Or so I've been told this is just one of the many reasons women love superhero movies.

We find our seats, which mechanically recline, and I reach for Annabelle's hand. The lights go dim as the previews start, and I lean over the armrest to whisper in her ear.

"If this were high school, I would try to make out with you the entire movie." My hand skims up her arm.

Anna pushes up on her elbow so that her lips reach my ear. "And if this were high school, I might even let you touch my boobs. But ... it isn't."

When I pull back from our hushed conversation, she's smirking at me. I'd meant to tease her, get her keyed up so that she would think about me kissing her the whole movie, but now I'm the one who has to hide my growing boner.

The previews end and the lights go completely out, and then the opening credits light up the room and I'm engrossed. I hold Annabelle's hand the whole movie, squeezing it periodically to let her know I'm glad I'm here with her. Or, at least I hope she can interrupt my hand squeezes that way.

This is nice, sharing a night out at the movie theater with her. A normal date in public, with no mention of our awkward past or the sexual tension that comes with watching her eat and drink across the table at dinner. I look over periodically at my girl, and I'm not surprised that she's not only watching, but seems to be invested in what's happening on the screen.

And the movie? Well, the movie is everything I thought it would be and more. Of course, it ends on a cliffhanger and I make Annabelle stay all the way through the credits to watch the twenty-second teaser scene. Surprisingly, she doesn't object.

As we walk to the car, hand in hand, she looks up at me. "Thanks for tonight. It was ... normal."

I laugh. "Are we not normal?"

She leans over so that I sling one arm around her shoulder, walking with her pressed against me. "We are, sort of. But, we both have crazy jobs that take so much out of us. And we're in the public eye, I know that you know we both get stopped on the street more than we'd like. But tonight was just so ... ordinary. It felt good to not have any expectations, to be able to be myself."

It's a hell of an admission coming from this normally closed-off woman, and I bend to kiss her cheek. "That's how I always want you to feel around me."

"And because tonight was very sweet, a la high school crushes, I will admit something."

I know what she's about to say, but I want the satisfaction of her speaking the words. "And what is that?"

She hangs her head in mock shame. "I really enjoyed the movie and I'm begging you to binge watch the individual character movies with me."

I pump a fist in the air. "I knew it! I knew you'd love it. And yes, I will rent a whole lineup of binge-worthy superhero movies for us this weekend. In between games and shoots, we'll watch the one about the aquatic superhero, the super-speed one, the normal guy who falls into a vat of acid—"

Annabelle cuts me off, laughing. "You're such a nerd."

A lot of people probably think I order all of my pieces or fabrics or decor from catalogues or online.

And those people would be wrong.

If only the viewers knew just how much time and energy went into picking the absolute best pieces for a project.

Wandering around the flea market an hour outside of Austin, I brush my fingers over old wooden armoires, sewing desks with actual spindles built into them, drapes from decades past and a whole other assortment of items that I could incorporate into the numerous projects I'm currently working on for James and Ramona.

That is my biggest strength, the golden talent I bring to the table. I can walk through places like this, or antique shops piled high with garbage, and pick out the diamond in the rough. I would give the house character, just with that one great piece. It would bring a story to the home, and it is my own personal addictive game to find the best fit of an item for each client.

"This place smells." Boone walks up, wiping a finger over a dusty old mirror.

"That's half the charm of it." I'm semi-ignoring him, my nose to the ground like a basset hound trying to find it's intended target.

When he agreed to come with me to the flea market, I'd been pleasantly surprised. In high school, everything was about him. His friends, his sport, his parties, what he wanted to talk about. He hadn't taken much of an interest in learning what I liked. But now, it seems like he is trying to get to know me on a deeper level. Plus, it's kind of sweet that he's committed to something very far out of his comfort zone just because he knows I enjoy it.

Boone's phone buzzes, and he falls behind, probably checking a text or something.

And because I am alone for a minute, I sneak a glance at my own phone, chewing on my lip.

I'd finally opened the contract that Kutch's office had sent over. It was more than generous. A huge salary, a pretty good benefits package with some creative control. But those were about the only positives. It also outlined the way I had to dress, skimpy for lack of a better word, how much I was allowed to say and which media outlets I'd have to be pimped out to. The network would have complete control of who was chosen to work on the show, and which clients I took on. There were certain words I was outlawed from saying on TV, and another team would have full approval on final designs. Meaning I couldn't even feature my own designs; I knew from experience that I'd be shot down at every turn for pieces or decor I wanted.

And the contract also featured a gag order on discussing any of this with Ramona and James. I have a feeling they included that because of the worst part of the entire stack of documents ...

My new show would be replacing *Hart & Home* in its time slot. My mentors would be downgraded to the earlier hour.

It stung every part of my body to read through the treachery of my contract. I actually had to stuff it back in its envelope after digesting it and threw it under a stack of papers so that I wouldn't have to think about it.

But at the same time, this is what I've been waiting for. My chance to breakout, to headline, to make my mother finally take notice. I couldn't not take this shot.

Which is why I'm standing in the middle of a dirt-infested flea market, working for someone else, staring at my mother's latest LinkedIn status about attending the biggest conference in her field this weekend. There is a picture of her, slender and powerful in her jet-black skirt and suit-jacket. She looks incredible, commanding, and cold as ice.

The exact picture of what I want to be. Because if I can be just like her, maybe she'll finally love me.

"What's that?" Boone peers over my shoulder.

Quickly, I click my phone so the screen goes black. "Nothing." I smile chastely. "I think I found it. That teal chest of drawers with the ornate etching of roses going across the top. Think you can carry it?"

He smirks, and I want to wipe it off his face with my own lips. "Ah, so that's why you brought me along."

"Let's see if that muscle is just for show, or ..."

Boone goes to walk past me, but bends and whispers in my ear, surprising me. "You know firsthand that none of this is for show."

His shoulder brushes mine and goose bumps break out over my skin, both from the contact and his confident words.

After paying, loading the *Hart & Home* truck we drove down here and stopping for gas, Boone finds us a hole in the wall restaurant off the highway that boasts the best grits in all of Texas. Too bad I don't like grits, but if it means more time with him, I'm not complaining.

We've been talking and hanging out, for lack of more mature words, for about two weeks now. With our crazy class and work schedules, it isn't easy. And there was still a lack of trust on his part and a standoffish nature on mine, but ... like we'd both said all along, there was still a spark. We have that undeniable *thing* that was not going to be found with anyone else, so we owed it to ourselves to try.

"So, you decided to link us publicly, huh?" I can't tell if he's pissed or if he enjoyed my video message.

Already, there were articles on five local Texas gossip sites. I hadn't really meant to make a statement with the video message, but when Ramona and James mentioned they had been asked to film it, I decided *what the hell*? Boone had always said that I had a block of ice on my shoulder, and I wanted to show him that I care. That I knew how important that moment was for him.

My stomach turns with unease. "I was wondering when this would come up. I figured I couldn't be at your first game and I wanted to do something special ... I'm sorry if it was too much."

I wasn't really sorry, because I was going to do what I wanted to do at any given moment, but I could apologize for making Boone feel uncomfortable if he was.

Boone's fingers played with mine on the table. "Nah, I guess I should get used to it. You always were pushing me outside of my comfort zone, what's one more stunt. Plus, I kind of liked your big face looming over my shoulder the whole game. It might have made me play better."

I smack his hand lightly. "Hey, I do not have a big face!"

Those caramel irises gaze at me. "No, you have the most beautiful face I've ever seen."

"God, that's so corny." I roll my eyes.

"Is that why you're blushing?" Ego radiates off him like he's won something.

I lie. "No, I just got overheated at the flea market."

"You're so full of shit. You like my compliments, and you're overheated sitting across from me." Boone smiles, puffing out his chest.

"Did you take some injection of ego today or something? Aren't you supposed to be a quiet one?"

His lips spread even wider. "Just have to give you a taste of your own medicine. You want to embarrass me at the ballpark, I'll make you blush all day, sweetheart."

"Order your grits before I decide to leave you here out of sheer annoyance." I flip my hair over my shoulder.

Boone just chuckles as we place our order, and I can't help but smile too.

Banter is just talking disguised as foreplay. And it looks like we're speaking the same language.

W hen I asked Annabelle if she wanted to come up after we'd dropped the flea market finds and van off at James and Ramona's storefront, I honestly hadn't meant for sex.

I had a fun day with her, and it was rare for both of us to have a day off, so I wanted to spend more time getting to know each other again.

But since I'd asked the question, it seemed like every single word spoken was charged with lust. It's woven in there between syllables, and every time we look at each other, I swear it's like we are imagining the other on their back.

"Do you want a drink or anything?" I ask her, even though I don't have a drop of alcohol in this place.

"No, thanks." Annabelle chews on her lip, looking around my apartment. "Your place is nice. Needs some soft blankets on the couch and maybe a hand-crafted wood bar, but I like what you've done with it."

I walk toward her where she stands in the middle of my living room. "I have to admit, it came mostly furnished. So this is the work of some decorator."

"I'm crushed you didn't ask me." She holds her hand to her chest, pouting. "I would have given you a friends and family discount."

Her sentence makes it sound like she still wants to give me that discount in another way. My cock twitches in my shorts.

We're standing in front of each other, and slowly our eyes circle around to meet and hold each other. I should have known this would happen if I brought her up here. Since we gave ourselves a fresh start, it was always coming to this.

"I'm not sure if we should do this tonight," I say honestly.

Annabelle nods. "I'm not sure we can't *not* do this tonight."

She's always up front about things, that's for sure. But she's right, no one is walking out right now. We're not going to sit on the couch and watch a show or stop at a kiss good night.

So I start there, knowing I won't be able to stop.

One of my hands cups her cheek, and the other goes to her waist, pulling her toward me. I feel her good hand on my arm, trying to hold herself up against me as the kisses become deeper, more urgent.

Her casted hand moves to my face, and we stop.

"Guess that's the least sexy thing ever." She smirks.

"There isn't anything you can do to make me think you aren't sexy." I tuck her hair behind her ear.

"Smooth line." Annabelle rolls those mocha eyes.

I catch her chin in my hand. "I'm not giving you a line. It's true. Why do you think I came back to you after all of these years? I can't stay away. You're irresistible to me."

Her eyes shine, and I'm about to ask if she's going to cry, but she plants her mouth on mine instead. My heart thumps against my chest, and not because she's mewling into my throat. I swear, she was about to show me what's underneath all of those walls she's built. For me, that's even sexier than anything we could possibly do in the next few hours.

And then she cups me over my shorts and I know that my last thought was completely wrong.

I pick Anna up, careful not to jostle her casted wrist too much. She straddles my waist, her core grinding into my hard, twitching dick as I hold her. Before long, I'm growling as she latches on my neck, and that raw male feeling that beats inside my chest when I'm fully turned-on is raging. I feel like I could break cement walls or jump out of a plane. It sounds stupid, childlike even, but when I'm with her, I feel invincible. That night in the car, when I was pounding in and out of her ... it was the most alive I've been in my entire adult life.

"Boone ..." My name is a plea on her lips.

Carrying her, I walk us toward the bedroom, her mouth roaming my face, setting my skin on fire. She is all curves and limbs around me, and if I don't get her naked in the next twelve seconds, I think I might just die.

Setting her gently on my bed, I peel of my clothes, the sweat and dirt of the day coming off with them. Annabelle watches me from her position, propped up on her elbows with her legs falling open on my comforter. The sundress she wore to the flea market is navy and white, and with her dark hair and olive skin, it makes her look like a Grecian princess.

"Take them off." I'd begun to climb onto the bed toward her when Annabelle instructs me.

I've left my boxers on, wanting to warm her up properly, to tease her and bring her right to the edge, before either of us focused on me. But, I wouldn't be with her if I wasn't aroused by her bossiness. So I do as I'm told, standing to push them past my hips, my cock springing free.

Her tongue darts out and licks her bottom lip as she stares, unashamed, at my straining, hard dick. "I didn't get to see it properly last time. The first time."

A twinge of guilt hits me square in the chest as I join her on the bed. "That wasn't how it should have been. I'm sorry."

Annabelle looks up at me as I settle over her. "I'm sorry, too. But, it looks like we have a do-over."

I wink. "In that case, I think I'll take my time. You know, to really appreciate everything I missed."

Sliding down her body, I don't bother taking the dress off yet. It's hot on her, the white fabric against her tan skin, and it's even hotter when I push it up past her waist, yank her underwear down, and bury my face in her pussy.

"Oh. My. God," she moans, writhing under my tongue.

Drinking her in, I ease the orgasm out of her, slowly so that I can memorize each sweet lick. Annabelle grips my hair, threads her fingers through it, kneads at the muscles on my arms that hold her in place so I can taste her.

She was right. There is no way I could hold back from this. This moment right here, in my bed with her, has been a long time coming. We tried to hate, tried to fight it, but it was no use.

Giving in to everything, I rise up, undressing her limp body as she mewls from the climax that just stole her muscle function and brain power. I scoot her up, sliding us both under the covers and reach for a condom from my bedside table. I want her under all of the sheets, wrapped close to me, our heat encasing us.

"Don't take your eyes off of me," I command.

Her brown pools lazily lock on mine, and I can see the drunk lust mirrored back at me. But in my case, that lust is laser-sharp. I feel like an animal about to devour its prey, methodically and slowly until I've won every part of her over.

Annabelle's slim arms loop around my neck, and the tip of my nose presses against hers.

And then, I slip inside of her tight, hot wetness.

"Fuck ..." I say quietly, gulping as if I'm being strangled.

I guess I am though, just much farther down than my neck. Her pussy is a vice, and the gripping feeling is so intense that I don't think I'll be able to hold out, even with how the condom blunts some of the sensation.

"I always knew ..." Annabelle trails off, and I forget that the last time, our first time, she was halfway down a tequila bottle.

I can't speak, because I fear that if I do, I'll say something stupid. Something that is altogether too fast for us.

So I just stare into her eyes as I work both of us to the brink of destruction.

I hope she understands everything I'm trying to convey with just my gaze.

"Let's go, Boone!" I shout at the top of my lungs.

"The cheerleader in her is coming out." Harper smirks at Cain.

Cain chuckles. "Nah, the cheerleader in her threatens random new girls and bakes cookies for football players. Oh, and tries to control how her teammates curl their hair. But the cheerleader in her definitely never actually rooted for the guys on the field."

I punch Cain in the leg. "I can still destroy you if I want to."

He pretends to cower in fear.

"Oh, fuck, that wasn't a strike." I bite my knuckles, my knees shaking as the batter before Boone is struck out.

I've been told, by both Harper and Boone, that I need to tone it down at the games. Apparently, me giving the umpire a tongue lashing last game from the stands is not looked upon favorably by my guy's coaches.

Boone steps into the batter's box, and I whistle around two fingers. He doesn't look up, and I know he's fully in the zone. I was on the receiving end of that focused gaze the other night in

Boone's bed ... and remembering that makes me shiver in the Texas heat.

Goddamn, he drives me insane. I can feel myself grow wet right here in the stadium seat as Boone takes a strike and a ball each.

"He's going to swing at this one." Cain leans forward in his seat.

It's sweet that those two have found a détente, although I won't lie, there is some dark satisfaction to men fighting over you. Even if they weren't really fighting over me ... and sweet? Who the hell have I become? God, I need to ream out a production assistant or something tomorrow.

Sure enough, Boone's muscled arms power his bat into the ball, hitting it with a sickening *thwack*. I wonder, for a second, as I watch it sail through the air if he's knocked the stuffing out of it.

Watching him play the sport he loves more than anything else on this planet ... I understand it. It might not be as highly regarded as professional sports, but I absolutely love what I do. The career I am building is the one I've dreamed of from a young age. I can't imagine what it is like for people who never get to live their passion ... and on some level I understand my mother in that regard.

But watching Boone, I can almost grasp why he'd been so one-minded when we'd dated in high school. He is a god on that field, his instincts and movements are perfectly attuned to every play.

We watch the rest of the game play out, and Boone's team wins in a close one-run victory that ends on a spectacular double play. The entire mood of the ballpark is jubilant.

It takes a while for Boone to join us at the player's exit, but when I see him, all dark and quiet confidence, my stomach dips and my heart beats twice as fast. This man affects me physically, he rearranges the way my body is supposed to function. The way I feel about him is molecular.

"Hey, you." He bends down to lay a gentle kiss on my lips, right there in front of everyone.

It takes me right back to that little girl, swooning over the tall, handsome senior.

"Who wants pizza?" Harper rubs her stomach.

Cain slings his arm around her shoulder. "Her love of food, it's why I love her."

Twenty minutes later, we pack into a corner booth at Salvatore's, the local pizza joint. It's a madhouse, with students and families everywhere, and we're lucky that we're with Boone and Cain, because a couple of people applaud loudly as we walk in and we're ushered to a semi-quiet area like we're VIPs or something.

Hell, I must be chopped liver because no one ever applauds when I walk into a restaurant, and I'm on television more than either of these two. I'd like to just say, *men*, and then mentally roll my eyes.

The waiter comes to take our order, and Cain asks for a round of beers.

"That's okay, I don't drink, water is fine with me." Boone waves the waiter off.

"You don't?" My eyebrows furrow in confusion.

"No, I haven't had a drink since I was seventeen. Which seems ironic, if you think about it. I quit alcohol before I could even legally have it." He chuckles.

Harper and Cain take this moment to talk to friends of Cain's over the back of the booth.

I lean into Boone. "But what about that night in your car? You were drunk." I am so confused.

"No I wasn't. You were really drunk. I was just horny."

Boone's teeth catch his bottom lip and I am momentarily distracted.

Which means that he'd slept with me of his own accord. Not that it hadn't been consensual on my part, but I don't think I would have had the courage to have sex with Boone if there weren't shots of tequila involved.

"Wait, so why did you stop drinking?" And now alarm bells are going off in my head.

I immensely respect those who have recovered from an addiction. But ... to bring that into a new relationship was difficult. I wouldn't know how to act if I wanted a glass of wine, I didn't know his triggers or whether or not it was still a struggle for him to be around any type of partying.

Boone touches my cheek, and it is like we are the only two people in this entire restaurant. "Relax, Anna. It wasn't because I couldn't handle myself. I just ..." He sighs now, and I know he is weighing whether or not to tell me the real answer. "My dad is basically a drunk, and watching him, I didn't want to end up that way. So, I just stopped."

A lump forms in my throat. "I ... I had no idea."

Because I really hadn't. Up until this moment, I'd been so consumed with my own baggage and ugly parental situation that I hadn't realized that the man I've been getting close to was sitting in the exact same boat as me. I look at Boone with fresh eyes; maybe this was why we'd come back together after all these years. Maybe deep down, each of us had identified with the pain in the other. Maybe, we share the same insecurities and can heal that in each other.

My pessimistic heart could hope.

"And now you do." He kisses my cheek and picks up a menu, which signals that he doesn't want to discuss it further. At least not here.

"All right, one pepperoni, one sausage, one meat lover's

supreme and one buffalo chicken?" Harper slams her menu down on the table.

"You'd think she was a Texas girl and not a transplant with all the meat she eats." I grin at my stepsister.

"You're just annoyed because I won't let you order a veggie pizza. Veggies on pizza defeats the entire point," Harper whines.

I snuggle into Boone, happy to have a night off with him, and warmed at the thought that he just shared something with me that he definitely withheld from most.

"As if you're going to stop me from doing anything I want to do." I smirk.

Boone laughs at this, setting his water down after taking a sip. "Big mistake, Harper. Never tell this one what she can and can't do. She'll do the opposite and then convince you you're the one who made the decision in the first place."

Well, he wasn't wrong about that.

Her LinkedIn page is pulled up again, and I thumb through it under the work table I am at.

I'm like someone stealing answers to a test, glancing down sneakily at my phone every few minutes and then back up to make sure I haven't been caught.

"Hey, darlin'." Ramona's voice echoes in the studio, and I nearly jump. "Whoops, didn't mean to scare you."

She comes around to where I am putting together inspiration boards for private clients, those who aren't going to be on the show. To be honest, these are my favorite projects. These kinds of clients usually have taste, money and a better eye for decor than those who sign up for TV only wanting to gain their fifteen minutes on the screen. Making their vision boards, pulling from Italian architecture or Swedish linens, it is quiet, thoughtful work and I love locking myself in the open-air design studio James built for Ramona. And the plus is that he renovated an old brick office building only five minutes from campus in downtown Austin, so I could come here whenever I like.

Quickly, I shove my phone into my bag. "Hey, what're you doing here?"

My tone sounds accusatory and nervous, and Ramona laughs slightly. "Am I not allowed to come to my own office?"

I roll my eyes. "Of course you are, sorry. I was just enjoying the quiet."

She thumbs through a couple of things on her desk and then looks up. "I can leave if you want me to."

"Don't be stupid, it's your place, you can do whatever you want." That came out harsher than I intend it to.

"Is something wrong?" She comes over to sit on the stool next to mine at the big steel table in the middle of the room.

Other than the fact that I'm entertaining an offer to knock your show down the ladder? Or that my mother hasn't cared about me in ten years? Or that I'm back together with the guy I cheated on and I'm walking on eggshells not to lose him again?

But I don't say any of those out loud. Because per usual, I want someone to care, but didn't want to let them in. Drama, as Boone would say.

"Why would you think that?"

"Honey, I've never said anything, but I know that there is some drama when it comes to your mama. You know that I am always an open ear whenever you need one, right?" She rubs my knee, her face so open and honest.

How the hell could I sit here, with a huge secret in my back pocket, and basically lie to her? This woman has done nothing but jumpstart my career, make me a part of her family, and given me every kind of support possible. And here I am with a contract sitting on my dorm room desk to basically bump her off the Flipping Channel.

I am a terrible fucking person.

So I go with the third problem in my life right now, because I need to tell her something. And, it will actually be helpful to talk to someone who doesn't know the history between Boone and me.

"Well, I've been kind of seeing someone ..." I scratch my nail at the steel table.

"It's Boone Graham, isn't it?" Her face goes all moony.

I give her a pointed look. "How did you know?"

She pats my shoulder and smiles. "Honey, I may be an old, married woman, but I know what it means when a man looks at you the way that Boone does. Like you hang the moon."

I can't help the blush that creeps onto my cheeks. "He does not look at me that way."

"Sweetheart, from the minute James fangirled over him in that stadium, I could see that boy was crazy about you. Don't be your usual ice princess-self and try to deny that." Her green eyes scold me.

"I just am not sure what we're doing," I confess, more to myself than to her.

"Well, what do you mean?" Her brows furrow.

I sigh, setting down the pen I'd been scrawling notes with. "We spend a lot of time together. I go to his games and some-times he texts me when he's caught an episode of the show. I ... spend nights at his place. He takes me out to dinner. But, we haven't had the talk yet. And he doesn't seem all that rushed to do so."

Ramona laughs. Tilts her head back and laughs some more. "Oh, darlin' ... didn't I tell you? Men are lazy, and they can be dumb as a box of bricks. I thought you knew better than to let them do the defining. Hell, when James and I were dating, I dragged him to the jewelry store, pointed out the ring I wanted, and told him he better not mess it up. I was not wearing an ugly bobble on my hand for the rest of my life!"

My mouth drops open. "See, I knew there was a dark side of you. Maybe you *are* more of a mother to me than I thought."

"Aw, I will be a mother figure to you any day, honey. But in all seriousness, forget etiquette and what Southern belles are supposed to do. If you want the man, claim him. Who cares? Wouldn't you rather be happy than be in purgatory?"

Her advice is honest and true, and I have never been one to sit back and let the things I want pass me by. Except when it came to Boone.

Ramona hugs me and gets up, going to sit at her desk and take a call from a marble distributor.

The one thing I hadn't told her, though, was that love is the one thing I couldn't go after and claim. I'd seen love, relationships and marriage completely destroy my mother and father. It had tied one down for too long, while the other was left heartbroken when it vanished.

I wasn't going to do that to myself. I wasn't going to be the one tied down, or the one left in pieces. No, if this was going to be solidified, if we were going to commit to a relationship, Boone was going to have to be the one to initiate it.

Otherwise, I'd be left vulnerable.

Otherwise, I would shatter if it ended. Again.

A month whizzes by when you are an athlete and a student, and not a hybrid but actually two separate people.

Sometimes, I feel as if I'm in a tornado, being whipped from one place to the next. A game in this city, an exam for this class, a group study with these people or a media day or charity event for the team.

I try to schedule phone calls with my mom for when we are on the bus driving to a game and studied for the last month of classes in between double headers.

Any spare time is reserved for Annabelle, and I feel like a dick that it is so little. I attempt to take her out at least one day a week, because it's important to me to court her. I was there when they removed her cast, and even bought her a nice bracelet to adorn her newly healed wrist. To make her feel special, to show her that this isn't a repeat of the closed-off, self-centered asshole I was in high school.

At some point along the way of us starting a new chapter, that chapter has turned into a relationship. It just happens that way, more often than not. A pattern becomes a routine, and then you're just in it with that other person, and you're a we instead of a me. I guess we should have a talk about it at some point but … I'm a guy. If I'm spending all my time with you, I'm with you. I don't understand the need for the titles or declaring our status on social media.

Tonight is a study session at my apartment, since finals are looming and graduation, for me, is on the horizon. My girl is lost deep in the large book she has open and is scrawling notes in a three-ring binder next to it. I should be concentrating on the trigonometry problems that have been stumping me all semester, but I can't stop looking at her.

Annabelle ditched out on a design expo last week to come to one of my games, because she's my new good luck charm. I averaged two home runs a game in the six games she's been able to make it to, and I don't realize that she's going to miss another day of class and shooting until she randomly blows up at me when I bring the trip this weekend up.

"Hey, make sure to pack a bathing suit this weekend, I'm pretty sure we can fit in a beach day since this team we're playing is so close to the ocean."

The design textbook she's reading suddenly slams down on the table. "So now you're telling me what to wear too?"

I've had a long day, and in the back of my head, I knew things were going too well. The dramatic side of Annabelle hasn't reared its ugly head in a while, and I knew it was lurking under the surface.

"What's the problem?" I huff, annoyed and tired.

"The problem is that ever since we started … you know, I'm not even sure what we're doing here! Yet again! How do I keep falling into this trap with you?"

The hair on my skin stands up and I can feel my blood pressure creep higher. Have I not been open with her? Have I not told her things and shared about myself? I've been trying so hard to do this right this time.

"So is this about a fucking bathing suit, or do you want to admit the real reason you're being a brat?" I walk out of the kitchen where I'd been cleaning a pot and try to restrain myself by crossing my arms.

"Don't curse at me, Boone Graham. Not when I'm the one making all the sacrifices here. I've missed days of shooting and class, rearranged my plans to see you whenever you're not on the road."

I throw my hands up, because she's being ridiculous. "I didn't ask you to do that! I thought you wanted to make us work! And it's not like I can just tell the team I'm going to sit this one out because I need to go on a date! Jesus, Anna."

"No, but you can call me your freaking girlfriend once in a while!" she screams, her voice reaching a pitch I haven't heard it get to before.

I'm so pissed off, I could spit nails. "Are we so immature that we have to ask each other to be girlfriend and boyfriend? For fuck's sake, yes, you're my girlfriend, okay?"

"Well don't sound so happy about it!" She jumps up from the couch and stomps toward the bathroom, slamming the door shut.

So she's pissed at me for not labeling us, but freaks out when I do actually call her my girlfriend? Women were so fucking dramatic.

I walk to the bathroom, the anger letting out of me like air from a balloon as I hear a sob from inside. Knocking, I try to make my voice soft. "Babe?"

It's the first time I've called her the nickname, but I want to use the endearment. I want her to know that yes, we are in a relationship.

After a minute, Anna opens the door. Her eyes are red, and

guilt fills my stomach. The last thing I ever want to do is make her cry.

"I'm not going to be some trophy wife on the arm of a ballplayer." She shrugs, not meeting my eyes.

Taking her hand, I lead her to the couch, where we sit down facing each other. I'm not going to wimp out of this discussion, and I'm going to force us both to be adults.

I sigh. "And I'm not asking you to. Just like you would never ask me to give up my career. I'm not the bad guy here, Anna. I'm trying to compromise. I wouldn't want to be with you if you weren't exactly the way you are. Maybe a bit too stubborn at times, but I want to be with you because you're so difficult. Sue me, I'm a masochist."

I can see the wheels going in her head, and I intervene. Moving in close, I slide my lips over hers, kissing her gently but in a steady rhythm. My goal is to get her out of that steel trap of a mind, to stop thinking, to stop internalizing all her fears for once.

When I can feel her panting breath on my lips between kisses, I pull back. "Talk to me. Stop creating scenarios in your head and just talk to me."

Anna has to look away to speak, but at least she's speaking. "Did you know that my mother left my dad and I when I was ten?"

Fuck. I'd always known something was up with her family situation, but I never asked back in high school. And I didn't want to pry now. "I didn't know the specifics."

She nods, and I do my best to look like I'm here for her as a sounding board. "I honestly don't know why she did. I've never had the closure to be able to talk to her about it. Although, that just might hurt too much to actually do. But ... I can sometimes understand it. My dad, he's great. But she was a stay-at-home housewife. For ten years, all she did was clean up after her family and drive me around and live under Dad's shadow. He's successful, a workaholic, and has gotten so many accolades in his job that it must have been hard for her. She must have felt ... just so much less. I never want to be like that. I never want to live behind someone else. I want to be independent, both emotionally and financially. I hate having to rely on someone."

My fingers tangle in her smooth chocolate locks. "I don't want you to rely on me. I want us to rely on each other. That's what a relationship is, Anna. Your mother was wrong for taking off like she did. If she felt like that, then she should have said something. I understand following your dreams but leaving those that love you behind is also completely wrong. By you just sitting here, opening up to me ... you will never become her. Because even though you didn't say it, I know that's what you're really scared of."

Her eyes search mine. "When you told me about your dad, part of me felt like we were cut from the same cloth."

I pick her up, all the way into my lap so that I can cradle her. "We are. And you are my girlfriend, even if you scream at me. I'm not leaving you, babe."

She tucks her head under my chin. "Thanks for putting up with my drama. I just ... need validation sometimes. And it's big of me to admit that, realize it. I want to let you in, but the way I was conditioned sometimes makes me freak out. You have to give me time."

"I'll give you all the time you need."

I gave a verbal commitment two weeks ago to the show that Kenneth Kutch had pitched me.

I lied and told his assistant, who'd been pestering me for the last month and a half about signing that foul contract they'd sent over, that my attorney was still looking it over.

But the truth is, I want to keep the offer on my plate while also deliberating with my conscience. Deep down, I know this isn't the right opportunity. The show would be gaudy and tacky, with clients that I'd hate even more than those I had to deal with on *Hart & Home*. On the other hand, though, it is just the right launching pad to get me recognized, make me infamous, and have a certain someone take notice.

I don't want to sign it, but that nagging feeling of never being good enough for my mother won't allow me to turn it down.

A mother shapes the very fabric of her child. What she does, or doesn't do, impacts the child's life forever. Did your mother pick at and critique every piece of food you put into your mouth? Then you probably have a complex about eating. Did your mother tell you who to be friends with and who not to be friends with, depending on their popularity? Then you are probably very distrusting. Did your mother constantly push you without the appropriate amount of pride expressed? Then you probably think you will never be good enough.

We all have mama drama. I know I'm not the only one. But it's a little bit different for me, because my mother left. She wasn't there to screw me up in other ways, because she simply wasn't there. And she didn't pass away either, which is another whole sorrow-filled set of issues that I wouldn't wish on anyone. No, mine actually decided that she didn't want to be a mother anymore.

And with that decision, she shaped the fabric of my life forever. I didn't have that love, or nagging, or pride, or fun, or tradition. I didn't have any of it. It's why I've been so socially stunted my entire life. I lack the warmth and vulnerability and qualities to get along with others because my mother showed me that by being closed off, by being alone, you could be successful. She'd done it with her career, by way of example.

But at some point, we have to get past all of the terrible things our parents did to us. Whether big or small, we have to learn the acceptance it takes to move on from those issues, because after all, our parents are just people. They don't have to be these gods and goddesses on that pedestal we put them on. They're just trying their best or practicing what they learned from their parents.

We can either stay mired down in their shit or rise above it and choose to change.

I am trying to choose to change. I've come so far, with the help of Harper and the mother figures in her life. And then with Boone in my life again, I am beginning to realize that I can have a moment of anxiety-filled panic, and he won't walk away from me.

Still, people don't change that quickly, if you even believed they could.

That's why I am at the Flipping Channel's offices on this Thursday afternoon, instead of in class. It's why I lied to Ramona and told her I was in bed sick, instead of at the reveal of a project we've been working hard on for three months.

It's why I am standing in front of a photographer in a skimpy red dress, pretending to "bring my sexy" and act like Rosie the Riveter in stilettos. Seriously, that is what this prick has asked me to do.

Kutch wanted promo shots to begin marketing the series once I sign the contract. These are nothing like what I had in mind. I look like a pageant queen in a trailer park dress, wielding a hammer like it's the biggest innuendo. The shots for my brand, that I had in mind, would feature a timeless Chanel suit, a well-placed overstuffed chair and some fabulous drapes as my background.

I could speak up, I could say no. But again, that LinkedIn page is burning a hole in the pocket of my bag that sits in the corner.

Sooner or later, I will have to make a decision one way or the other. I know either one will set the course for the rest of my career.

So for now, I let the pain in my heart, put there by my mother, rule my life.

"This is our one day off together for the next three weeks. Can't we just sit on the couch and eat ice cream? I told you I'd even watch another superhero movie!"

I'm whining, I know it, but it's because I truly mean what I say. Our schedules don't link up often so that we have an entire twenty-four hours of lazy freedom, but today they did.

And Boone wants to spend that time driving out to the country for God knows what.

"You'll like this better. I promise." His hand reaches across the gear shift and rubs up and down my thigh, eliciting tingles.

We've driven for almost an hour on the highway out of Austin before Boone takes an exit, winding through suburbs that turn into farmland and then eventually lead out to roads that might as well not even reside on maps.

"Where the heck are we?" I wonder aloud while entranced by the beautiful landscape whizzing past the car windows.

Boone doesn't say much the entire drive, just hums along to Kenny Chesney on the radio and holds my hand. When he finally puts the car into park, we're in a secluded gravel parking lot under a forest of trees.

"Let me guess, you brought me out here to murder me. Finally, off with my head!"

Boone chuckles, unbuckling his seatbelt. "If I wanted to kill you, I'd have done it a long time ago. I like you now, remember?"

Yeah, I remember. Especially since most of our alone, together time is spent sans clothes.

He takes a bag out of the back, grabs my hand as I get out of the car, and starts us walking. I don't ask where we are again, because I have a feeling my quiet man just wants to show rather than tell.

The lush forest of trees breaks about twenty minutes into our hike-walk, and I'm flabbergasted.

A waterfall, bigger than one I've ever seen, stands right in front of us. It runs down the side of an enormous mountain, blue and green water running off into natural rock pools and moving farther into the forest in streams and rivers.

"Wow," I breath, struck by the sheer beauty of nature.

While I can hang with the best of them on a construction site, I'm not much of an outdoors girl. Although I love the beach and the occasional run around the city. But this is breathtaking.

"Right? I saw pictures on a friend's Instagram of this place and thought it would be worth a trip out of the city." He shoulders the backpack he's taken out of the car.

"Well, I'm glad you at least told me to wear sneakers today."

"I just thought that a hike might be fun. A little exercise, a little sightseeing, a relaxing way to spend our day off." He bends over to kiss me, and it lasts longer than either of us probably intend it to.

Boone pulls back, smiling like a goof. "All right, let's go."

Usually, I'm an indoor gym kind of girl. But the nature preserve and falls he's brought me to is so gorgeous, I don't even notice we're exerting so much energy until we come to the large natural pool on the opposite side of the canyon we were hiking.

My legs burn, and my lungs are puffing out air, but it feels amazing. He was right, this was better than sitting on the couch. And it meant I got to watch his ass as he climbed in those workout shorts, and that is *way* better than any Netflix show I could binge.

Boone stops in front of the natural pool and begins removing his shoes.

"I didn't bring a bathing suit." Dammit, and cooling off in this beautiful place would have been great after the long week I've had.

He sets the backpack down. "It's a good thing I had Harper raid your dorm room then."

I'm a little shocked. "You packed for me?"

"I wanted it to be a surprise." He shrugs. "Let's see what we've got in here."

He riffles through the bag, pulling out a bikini for me, a swimsuit for him, two waters, a couple of Tupperware containers of food, and sunscreen.

"You're kidding. I'm ... very impressed." I raise an eyebrow at him, and walk over, wrapping my arms around him.

Going up on my toes, I hug him. Just hug him. The gesture is intimate and satisfying, to just be held by someone I care so much about it.

"Now I'm going over behind this rock to change. Don't sneak a peek," I scold him, holding a finger up.

"I've buried my tongue in your pussy, you don't think you can change in front of me?" He rolls his eyes.

My legs turn to jelly when those crude words come out of his mouth. I can't even speak, so I just pick up the bikini and walk to the rock to change.

Once I'm in my bathing suit, I walk out to find Boone already floating around in the pool. "Feels so good in here."

I don't hesitate, just run and jump, the water coming up at me fast. My body hits the surface, breaking the water into cool waves around me as I sink. The water tastes so fresh, the serene silence of being under calming my mind. Coming back up, I wade to Boone and splash him.

We swim for what feels like forever, challenging each other to see how long we can hold our breath, or do a handstand in the shallow part of the pool.

At one point, I get out, attempting to execute a dive.

"Bet you won't take off your top." Boone's expression is all challenge.

I'm no chicken, so I untie it, letting the triangles fall. "Oh, I won't?"

"You're so ballsy. Never the kind of girl to back off a dare. I love that about you."

My heart flutters, he said the word love. I bite back that feeling of hope. "Now you take your suit off."

His torso is under the water, and I watch as he removes them, throwing them over the side of the stones lining the pool.

"Now your bottoms." Those whiskey-colored eyes are heated.

"Fine, I'll take it off. But if I give you this, you have to agree to the second part of this date." I cock an eyebrow at him.

Boone folds his arms over his naked chest. "And what's that?"

"Nope, you didn't tell me where you were taking me, so I don't have to tell you. You just have to agree." My fingers dig into my bikini bottoms, toying with him.

His eyes go straight to the place where I'm about to push the skimpy piece of clothing from. "You know I'm the one driving, right?"

"Do you want me to take my clothes off or not?"

That gives him the kick in the ass he needs. "I agree. Now take those off and get in here, the water feels fine."

I 'd seen the place as we drove through the country, and I knew right away what it was.

Thankfully, I wore jean shorts and sneakers for our outing today, although cowboy boots would have been a better fit for this place.

You can hear the country music from the road, before we even pull into the parking lot. The sign, blinking yellow neon, is just one word, *Boots*.

After the hike today, I am starving and in desperate need of a stiff drink. Nothing like Texas barbecue, line dancing and beer to fix that.

We spent a good long while under that waterfall, kissing and touching and splashing water at each other. We were like kids in puppy love, daring each other with our tongues to go just a little bit further. It was all foreplay and teasing, and it made me feel lighter than I had in years.

"This is where you wanted to go?" Boone smiles at me from the driver's seat.

"We may be city kids now, but let's not forget that we grew up in the country." I wink at him, hopping out of the car.

Our fingers intertwine as we walk to the entrance, and there are two of three people standing outside the front door of the dance hall smoking cigarettes.

Inside, the place is electric. Booming music, the smell of fried food, beer and smoke. People laughing and singing, line dancing down the floor. It's a big, comfortable party, completely Southern style.

The hostess escorts us to a booth alongside the dance floor, and we marvel as the dancers stomp and twist, every single person knowing the steps to that particular dance.

Our waiter comes over and asks if we'd like a beer or a glass of wine.

Boone shakes his head at a drink, sticking with water, but I ask for whatever light beer they have on tap.

"Beer, huh? You're getting real honky-tonk tonight."

I smile at him, my eyes casting over to the dance floor. "One of my favorite memories of when my mom was still around is when we'd go to the Town Hall Dance in Haven. Remember it? They'd shut down Main Street and set up that big tent in the middle of town. And all of the moms and dads would two-step and slow dance together. I remember my father twirling her around out there, her smile so wide, and he couldn't keep his eyes off of her ..." I trail off.

When I look back at Boone, there is sympathy in his caramel eyes. "You don't talk about her much."

I shrug. "It's one of the only good memories of her that I have left."

"I'm glad we can make new memories." He looks at me, his eyes conveying something deeper. "There was a time, early on this year, that I wasn't sure I'd ever be able to look at you, truthfully. But I'm glad that we could both resolve the issues we had, both internally and with each other. I know I was an asshole, and you weren't a peach. But days like today ... I'll never forget that."

And you said you loved me today. I think it before I can correct myself. No, he said he loved that *about* me. I couldn't forget those details, I couldn't let my heart get ahead of my brain.

"Me too. Even if you're too good-looking for your own good." I smirk, because he looks damn good all sun kissed from the hike and windblown from the drive.

We order a whole bunch of food; corn bread and sweet pota-
toes, fried chicken, beef brisket and ribs slathered in chipotle
sauce. It's a messy feast, and while I'm usually a vapid salad and
smoothie kind of woman, I chow down. I see Boone smile at me
across the table a couple of times, but I'm too hungry to stop and
talk.

When we're done, we sit back, hands on our stomachs,
content and tired. Until ... a particular song comes on.

"Short Skirt Weather" by Kane Brown starts to beat over the
dance floor, and I give Boone a sassy smile. Trailing him by the
hand, I make my way to the dance floor. When we get there, he
lets me go, watching with a satisfied smile as I join the line of
dancers.

My body lets go of all the tension, of all of the anxiety. I'm in
a place where no one knows me, or at least if they recognize me,
they don't say it. I'm just another faceless dancer, and I let the
beat take me over.

My legs vibrate from the way I stomp my feet into the dusty
floor, swinging my hips in an exaggerated motion, following the
choreographed steps of the line dance that the entire floor is
following. It's fun and carefree, and I can't remember the last
time I just let go. Even when I went out on the weekends, it was
always about impressing someone or getting plastered enough
that I could forget about the negative thoughts that always lurk
in the back of my mind.

The song winds to an end, and "*Back to Life*" by Rascal Flatts
croons over the heads of the dancers. Boone slowly walks onto
the dance floor from where he's been standing, watching me, on
the sidelines.

Doesn't matter what we're listening to,
Spinning her around the living room,
And I fall apart every time.

Their lyrics make a knot form in my throat as the man I fell for back in high school wraps his arms around my waist and sways me across the dance floor.

"Thank you for today," I whisper in his ear.

His only response is to pull me closer until our cheeks press together.

"I so needed this today."

Harper picks up her second cappuccino of the morning, and I can't help but laugh.

"Um, you're going to put yourself into a caffeine coma, slow down." I pick up my own coffee and revel in the delicious energy of it.

"A caffeine coma is an oxymoron." She scowls.

"Not when your give yourself a stroke from one too many coffees." I shrug.

We're sitting in a corner booth at the diner closest to campus. It's our monthly sisterly bonding breakfast, something Harper instituted because she felt bad always being out of town. And when she was in town, she was usually holed up in her bedroom with Cain, and I was not about to interrupt that shit. So we'd agreed on a monthly brunch session, to fill each other in and call each other out on bullshit. Mostly, it was me poking holes in Harper's latest novels, and she would get on me about every life decision. She was the one person who could be just as mean to me as I was to her, and we still enjoyed our French toast in the process.

"Did I tell you that I'm starting a new book? This one is going to be a romantic suspense novel." Harper picks up a piece of bacon from one of the plates our waitress just set down and chomps a big piece into her mouth.

The table looks like it's the spread from a Harry Potter movie, you know the scenes in the Great Hall where all of the food just keeps magically piling up. I ordered French toast, hash browns, two scrambled eggs, a coffee and an orange juice. Harper opted for chocolate chip pancakes, bacon *and* sausage, and two sunny-side up eggs. Oh, and her cappuccinos with a side of apple juice. The other agreement for this breakfast is that we stuff ourselves with all of the food we avoided on our perpetually slipping diets.

"Hmm, romance. Interesting. Didn't peg you as a sexy smut kind of writer, but I'm all for it. As long as you get kinky in the sex scenes. Every woman loves a good fucking, don't let anyone tell you otherwise."

Harper's face flushes a deep pink at the word fucking. "You're so vulgar."

"Nah, just honest." I shrug, squirting ketchup on my eggs.

Except I wasn't honest. Not about the biggest lie of omission I was keeping from everyone. I still hadn't decided what to do about the show offer, and even though this breakfast has always been a safe vent space ... something was keeping me from telling my stepsister. Probably because I know she is my biggest and best mirror. Harper would tell me how much of an idiot I am being and to call them up right now and decline.

"Well, maybe you can give me some notes on your sex life with Boone, then." She waggles her eyebrows and I know she's just trying to get back at me for using the word fucking.

"Yuck. You know that sex is the one topic that is off-limits. It's like ... incestuous." I shudder.

"We're not even blood relatives. Before our parents got

married two years ago, we barely knew each other. That can't be incestuous." Harper rolls her eyes.

"Fine. Do you want to lay out all the details of your sex life with Cain?" I hit her where it hurts.

She relents. "Ugh, no. Fine, you made your point. But things are going well with you two?"

"Better than well. So much better that—" I don't want to say the words out loud for fear that they might come true.

"So much better that you're afraid it'll all come crashing down at some point." She pops a piece of runny egg yolk in her mouth as if she didn't just steal my thought.

I point my fork at her. "Why do we always think like that? Are we so afraid of being happy that we plan for the worst? It's like, I constantly think about what it would be like if someone I love died."

"Well, that's morbid. Hope it's not me." Harper snorts.

"No, I'm serious. I always think about what measures I'd have to take, if say, knock on wood, my dad kicked it. Would I have to go through his things? Sort through a will? Who would get his collection of rare coins? What would I have to split up with your mom? This is the shit I think about. My head is a fucked-up nightmare of scenarios."

Harper takes a sip of her cappuccino. "Nah, you're not. You're just brutal enough to admit it, unlike the rest of us. I think about that sometimes with Cain. Would I get kicked out of the apartment? We're not married, so I wouldn't get any of his money. Not that I want it, because mama makes money of her own. But you know what I mean … it's weird stuff to think about."

I nod, spearing a cut up piece of French toast. "How'd we get so off topic? Anyway, it feels like I'm waiting for the other shoe to drop or something."

"Stop doing that. I'm telling you now, woman-to-woman, you'll drive yourself insane. I used to do the same thing."

"Before you were old and married," I tease her.

"Yeah, yeah. But I did. That doubt as a woman, that we're not good enough, it's innate. If you constantly listen to that voice, bad things will happen. That shoe will drop. Because you're the one not confident enough in yourself to believe that you deserve all of the good things in your life. So stop doing it. We should all stop doing it."

Harper's words speak to me on a deeper level than she even probably knows. They make me pause, mid-chew, and digest the knowledge she's laying flat out on the breakfast table.

I resume eating. "You know, you're pretty damn good with words. You should write a book or something."

Harper chuckles. "Funny you should say that."

Just then, we hear the door of the diner bang shut and a creature makes its way to our table.

"You look like hell," I say to Thea as I scoot over so she can sit.

She flops down in the booth. "That's what seven whiskey sours will do to you."

With Harper's permission, I invited Thea to the second half of our breakfast this morning. I've been neglecting the friendship there since I've been spending so much free time with Boone, and I know that Harper likes my prickly, vulgar friend. Plus, Thea needs help with one of the finals in our classes and we were headed to the library after this. I would never get her there if I didn't trick her with the allure of greasy breakfast food first.

Despite popular belief, I really do care what is happening with the people I feel closest to. I might bust their balls or bitch at them, but I care if Harper is having a tough time flushing out a book idea. I care if Thea passes a test. And I'll help them succeed in anything they need help with, because that's just who I am. Loyalty has become a badge of spite I wear proudly upon my chest; if you matter to me, I am going to do everything in my power to help you because I've been betrayed and abandoned before and I was not going to do that to someone else.

Except you are, the little voice of my conscience whispers. Oh, just shut the fuck up, would you? I get to be loyal to myself too and have a couple moments to waver back and forth on getting my ultimate revenge on that woman. Because that's what my own show would be: the ultimate fuck you to my mother.

"I have like one beer and I'm hammered. I don't know how you keep doing it, nor do I think I personally want to find out." Harper chuckles at Thea's misfortune.

Thea scowls. "Keep laughing, Mrs. Kent. Not everyone can have a big dick and a nice set of abs to come home to every night."

"Well, I will say, it's a plus," I cut in, smiling like a Cheshire cat.

"Yeah, yeah, shut it you two lovebirds. I'll represent the disenfranchised single ladies over here." She steals a piece of Harper's bacon and earns a death stare.

I put a small plate together for her out of my sampling of foods. "Yeah, but it's like that saying, 'you always want what you don't have.' Like, I envy your curly, can-be-styled-any-way hair, while I have to live with mine straight as a pin. Or people who have big boobs always wanting little ones and vice versa. It's the same with being single or in a relationship. There are aspects of both that you miss if you have the other. I really love being in a relationship right now, but part of me envies your drunken mess of a night out."

Thea nods vigorously. "Yeah, like, I'd like a consistent hookup partner, I won't say the word boyfriend because that makes me a little nauseous. But I do love trolling for random cock."

Harper snorts into her coffee. "Jesus, I feel like I need to go to church being with you two."

"Oh, come on, this is a vent space. Spill it." I raise an eyebrow at her.

She sighs. "Okay, I'll admit that while I love Cain, I never dated anyone else. I never even kissed anyone else. Sometimes I wonder what it would be like to experience those things for the first time again with someone else. It must be ... exciting to experience different people."

Thea's smile is smutty. "Hell yeah it is."

"But you love Cain and would never do that," I point out. "It's just that we always think the grass could be greener."

Harper nods, shrugging. "A human flaw, I suppose."

"No, the grass is always greener. Sometimes it's even tan, or pale if I'm feeling freaky. And if I'm feeling downright dirty, that grass is uncircumcised." Thea giggles wickedly.

"Oh my God." Harper practically chokes on her apple juice.

I just laugh my ass off. There is no place like a girl brunch.

"So, I have an idea."

Annabelle walks toward me, a slinky silk nightgown slithering around her body. When the hell did she manage to put that on without me noticing?

I gulp, feeling lost for words. "Huh?"

She chuckles, noticing my visible distraction. "I said, I have an idea."

Sitting up a little straighter from where I am lounging on the couch watching a replay of the movie *Gladiator*, I'm all ears. "I have a lot of ideas right now. Where'd you find that little number?"

"Just a treat I packed in my overnight bag." She takes her time making her way over to me, letting me really look at her.

She sleeps over anywhere from three to four nights a week, and while I know we both like her being here, I have a feeling that part of her motivation is sleeping in a bed more comfortable than the one in her dorm room. But, I don't mind, if it means I get to circle her waist with my arm at the end of the night and wake up to all of that soft, chocolate-colored hair in the morning.

It surprised me just how quickly the feelings of resentment and hurt toward her could disappear. Yes, we are still building that trust together, but I'm not angry every time I look at her anymore. Laughter and sarcasm rule our dates, and the other day, she kissed my cheek in public for no reason at all. I am finding that Annabelle is a softer person than she tries to convince everyone she isn't.

"We're going to sit here and drink this bottle of wine together. Not in a bar, not in haste, just simply relaxing at home with a drink. Because just like you told me that I'll never be my mother, I'm going to show you that you'll never be your father."

She pours the blood red liquid into the two stemless glasses on my coffee table, the curve of her back as she bends over them way more interesting than the alcohol she's trying to push on me.

"I told you, I don't drink."

Annabelle rolls her eyes. "That's a self-imposed celibacy. And we both know that when you're around me, you can't hold out for long."

She lets the sentence linger in the air as she raises an eyebrow. I grab for her, sprawling her on top of me until she's straddling my sweatpants-clad lap. I can already feel my cock start to harden.

"Uh-uh. Drinking first, kissing second." She leans back, exposing a strip of gorgeous thigh as she grabs a glass off the table.

Still in my lap, Anna takes a sip and leans into me, swallowing. Her lips come down over mine, so slow and teasing that I growl.

But when our mouths actually meet, she slips her tongue inside. And I taste it. That musky, earthy, buzzing flavor of wine. It suffuses my tongue, crackling as Annabelle kisses me. It's erotic and heady, my body begins to tingle with the anticipation of another sip and her body grinding against mine.

Should I allow her to do this? Should I let myself slip down this rabbit hole? I honestly don't know what will happen. I haven't had a drink as a legal adult, and now my self-imposed celibacy, as Annabelle calls it, seems stupid. Why did I assume that if I had a beer or two, I'd turn into the chump that my father is?

This woman is showing me every day that she wouldn't become her mother by being vulnerable and allowing me to see the softer side of her. I could try doing the same thing. I could prove to myself that I didn't have to abstain from anything to avoid becoming the thing I feared the most.

"Mm, what kind of wine is it?" I have little to no experience with any kind of wine.

Annabelle bites my lobe gently as she speaks into my ear. "Cabernet. Full bodied, dark red ... gives off notes of chocolate and oak."

She could very well be telling me that she wanted to suck my dick while I pulled on her hair, that's how much that sentence about wine turns me on.

"Give me another taste," I growl into her neck.

She tips the glass to my lips, and I take a full sip on my own this time. It leaves my mouth wet and dry all at the same time, and the sting of the alcohol in my nose goes right to my head. I hold onto Annabelle for support, even though she's the one straddling me.

"I think this is just a ploy to take advantage of me." I capture her lips in mine, plunging my tongue into her mouth so she can taste the wine on my tongue.

Pulling away, she shrugs out of both slinky straps of the nightgown, revealing her breasts.

"Mmm." I grunt in appreciation, my hands coming up to

knead them as she tilts her head back, finishing the last sip of wine.

"More?" she asks.

I bend forward, popping one of her nipples in my mouth. "Oh, yes. Much more."

Sucking, biting with my mouth and squeezing her breasts in my hands leads to Annabelle coming undone on top of me. She's grinding me *hard*, so hard that I might just come in my sweatpants. I'm drunk on her and the few sips of wine I've had ... the effect of not having a drop of alcohol in five years.

Annabelle slinks off my lap, shedding her nightgown as she does. And then she's standing in front of me, completely naked, long hair falling down over her shoulders and past her breasts.

"Fuck, baby, you weren't wearing underwear this whole time? You're cruel." I bite my fist.

She smirks and pours more wine into the glass. Swaying in front of me, all curves and seduction, she takes a sip and passes it to me. As I let another gulp of the red liquid glide down my throat, I feel her removing my sweatpants and boxers. When my dick is released, hard as a steel pipe, and hits the air, I hiss, choking on the tail end of my sip.

And then my windpipe nearly collapses as she takes me in her mouth and cups my balls at the same time.

"*Holy shit*," I growl, gripping the back of the couch.

Annabelle works me in her mouth, bobbing her head up and down, lubricating my cock. When I know I won't last much longer, I pull her chin up.

"Ride me. Straddle my dick and make us both come."

Her eyes go molten with desire. She prowls up my body, panting, and I practically pull her up to sit at the head of my cock. The wine, her naked body, my adrenaline ... everything right now is at a boiling point and I can't wait anymore.

And then this woman, this beautiful creature, is sheathing

herself on me, throwing her head back, and moaning. I can do nothing else but hold on and watch her, admire the way her hips move, and her breasts bounce in front of me. She's radiant, completely free and has abandoned all logical thought.

"My God ..." I say in awe.

"I know, I know," Annabelle chants.

She thinks I'm talking about the sex, which is phenomenal. But I'm not. I can't get over the way she looks, I'll never forget the expression of pure bliss on her face. Just a couple of weeks ago we were fighting about if we were actually a couple. And now, once again, this woman has made me fall head over heels in love without any effort at all.

Some people are just drawn to others, with no explanation or time gone by. Annabelle is like that for me. An instant kind of thing, like alcohol after a long dry spell. She invades my blood, makes me dizzy, convinces me I'll never get enough of her.

"I'm going to—" Annabelle stills, my cock completely inside her.

Her pussy convulses, ringing me dry. It sets off my own climax, and all I can do is grip the couch behind me as I shoot my come deep inside of her.

After our orgasms rob us of muscle control, she collapses against me, and I stroke her hair against her damp back. And then my blood freezes.

"I forgot a condom." I've never done that before. I've always been super safe when it comes to sex, I wasn't trying to end my life before it started.

Annabelle doesn't even move. "Don't worry about it, stud. I'm on the pill, and if you know anything about me, it's that I'm diligent to a fault."

I let out a chuckle, which is hard even now. She's taken everything out of me. "You didn't want to tell me that I could go bare inside of you before?"

Anna kisses my neck, and just like that, I begin to harden inside of her. "I wanted to make you work for it."

My energy is back, just like that. I flip her sideways, onto her back, and come down on top of her. "I'll show you how hard I can work."

Annabelle responds with an excited giggle.

Aside from baseball and college graduation, I haven't let myself think too much about what I want my future to look like.

A house, marriage, kids ... they all seem like such far-off ideas. Things that would be there when I was ready, whenever that was.

But as we pull up to Ramona and James' refurbished farmhouse, an image of Annabelle and I in a house of our own with a little tike running around pops into my head.

Where the hell did that come from?

Honestly, I don't even know if I want kids. After what I've been through with my dad, even before he lost his job ... I don't know what kind of father I'd make.

I wonder, for just a moment, if Annabelle believes in marriage and kids after all she's been through as well.

"Hey y'all!" Ramona stands on the porch with a little girl and a little boy, waving madly.

"Anna!" The little girl runs down the set of white-washed wood steps, catching Annabelle around the waist in a big hug.

Anna lets out a puff of air. "Jeez, kid, you're gonna crush me one of these times."

An involuntary smile paints my lips at this child's obvious excitement over my girlfriend. I never thought of her as the kid type, but it's clear in just a few seconds that Ramona's daughter adores her.

Two more boys run out onto the porch, and my jaw unhinges a little. Four kids! I can't even fathom taking care of one little life, let alone four.

Annabelle points to me. "Guys, this is Boone. Boone, this is Gabby, Ethan, Connor, and Justin."

Gabby eyes me. "Is he your boyyyyfriend?"

She draws out the word, and I feel judged. By a kid. It's amazing how insecure tiny little voices can make you.

"I am." I puff out my chest a little, trying to look worthy.

"She's too pretty for you." Ethan, the oldest boy, looks at me with visible jealousy.

Annabelle kneels next to him. "I agree, E. You know you're the handsomest guy in the room."

And my heart melts. Because this woman, who is usually as warm as an ice cube, is being so soft and nice to this little boy who clearly has a crush on her.

He blushes, and she fist bumps him. It's a sweet surprise to see her so amiable toward these kids who clearly have spent a lot of time with her.

"Anna, Boone, thanks for coming!" James stands on the porch, an apron reading Kiss the Cook hanging around his neck.

"I only came because Ramona promised to make her spicy potato salad," Anna says, and by the tone of her voice, I can tell she's not joking.

"And for us!" Justin, the youngest and clearly only about four or five, pulls on the hem of her dress.

"Fine, for you!" She chases after all of them like a zombie or something, and they run, screaming with glee.

I walk up onto the porch of their gorgeous house and think to myself that a place like this wouldn't be so bad someday. Outside of the city, back to my small town roots, enough room to get a big old basset hound and fill it with a family.

It occurs to me that I've never once thought about my future in terms of a personal life, until right now. Until I saw Annabelle running around with kids at her feet.

"She's pretty great with them, huh?" Ramona gives me a hug in greeting.

I pull back. "She is. I have to say, I'm surprised. Anna doesn't strike me as a kid person."

"I think that there is a lot that our girl likes to disguise about herself. Those kids cracked her the first day she came to visit us at home. They had her down on the floor coloring in half an hour flat." We watch through the big bay windows all around the first floor of the house as Annabelle and James start to taste test all of the food.

Ramona chuckles. "We better get in there before those two eat all of our supper."

The inside of the house is even better than the outside, which is saying something. Outside, I find out, they have almost twenty acres of land that includes a vintage, hand-laid tile swimming pool that Annabelle can't stop talking about. They also have a barn complete with goats, sheep and four horses. The kids help out, which teaches them each valuable life lessons, and they often go to set with their mom and dad to learn the business. Connor seems to particularly idolize his dad and has asked for a tool box for his upcoming ninth birthday.

The Hart's house is a home, the exact kind you envision growing up in as a child. There are more windows than walls, it's all whites and pale blues and sturdy wood but playful decor.

The kitchen table is like an upgraded picnic bench setup, and Ramona has touches of genius DIY and design all around. Before we begin eating dinner, they say grace and then go around the table and say their thorn and their rose. This exercise lets each person tell the table what's the best and worst part of their day.

And the spread they have ... my God. Grilled chicken and ribs, which are fresh poultry and grass-fed animals from a local friend's farm. Fresh corn, creamed spinach, sweet potato dumplings and the spicy potato salad that definitely doesn't disappoint.

"Boone, what is your thorn and rose?" Gabby asks, eyeing me like she still doesn't know if she can trust me yet.

My eyes flick up to the ceiling, and I think for a minute. "Hm, well, my thorn would be losing my baseball game yesterday. It broke our six-game winning streak. But I think I can forget all about that, since my rose is being here with you all. I'm glad I could finally spend some time with your mom and dad and meet you all."

The little girl looks to be satisfied by this answer. She turns to Annabelle. "Okay, I approve. You can keep him."

All of the adults at the table laugh, and Anna nods her head. "Why thank you. I was afraid I'd have to get rid of him after tonight."

"I watched one of your games on TV with my dad. Can we play catch some time?" Ethan asks me, and this kid looks like he is so nervous to address me.

"Of course, bud. Hey, why don't you get your glove now?" I was so full from the feast I'd just chowed down on, and exercise was my vice.

"Mom, Dad, can I please be excused?" Ethan jumps up and down in his chair.

Ramona smiles, and James gives him a thumbs-up. "Go ahead, E, I'll go get my glove and come out with you as well."

James and I push back from the table, and I bend down to plant a kiss on Anna's head before I walk out.

"Give him hell, E!" Anna calls from behind us.

We toss around for a while, me giving the kid pointers as James throws back and forth between the two of us, looking as gleeful as his son.

"This is just too cool. I'm a fan, man." He smiles at me.

"*I'm* the fan, genuinely. What you do in there," I nod at the house, "is more than anything I've ever accomplished."

He gazes at Ethan. "Won't argue with that. They're the real lights of my life. Everything else, it just doesn't matter all that much when you have a family."

Ethan looks beat after forty minutes or so of playing catch and asks to go in and watch the hour of TV the kids are allowed a day. James grants him that, and we sit down on the front steps of the wrap-around porch.

"How do you juggle it all? The show, the family, your own personal happiness? I just ... sometimes when I think about pleasing Anna, baseball, school, it all just overwhelms me."

James sighs, looking out at the setting sun. "I met Ramona when I was fifteen. Right then, I knew she was the girl for me. We got married when we were nineteen, with a dream of owning a contracting and design business in our hometown. All of that got put on hold when we got pregnant with Gabby a month after our wedding. I had to go to work for someone else; Ramona took a secretary job at the local school. And the kids just kept coming. Bills and crappy apartments, we've seen some hard times, Boone. And now I'm not saying that you haven't worked for what you got, but I'll challenge anyone who says my wife and I ain't broken our backs working for what we got. It took us a long time to build our success. But the one thing that was always a constant was our family. It's why I've been able to build a strong business. There is nothing like the support of a strong woman and the children you created to get you through hard times. They're the sugar behind all of it. My success is not my greatest achievement. My family is."

His advice sits in my heart, swirling around the organ although I don't quite grasp all of it yet. He's older, far wiser than I am. I'm just at the beginning. I know what hard work is like, and I've struggled, but I've done it primarily on my own.

What would it be like to have the support of a partner for the rest of your life? What must it be like to come home and wash off all the disappointment of the day when you saw your kid's faces?

"Like I said, I'm a true fan. Not a lot of people stay as grounded as you and Ramona. It's refreshing."

He pats my knee and stands. "We should get back. Ramona made double chocolate chip cookies for dessert. But, if you ever need a dose of reality, come on over. We're always here with chores and homework for you to help out with."

"Deal." I shake his hand.

When I came here tonight, I had no idea that this family, and seeing Annabelle with them, would make me have even more things to consider when it comes to my future.

But here I am, picturing my life in ten years. And I'm not surprised to see Annabelle by my side.

"Where is he? I can't spot him yet!"

Boone's mom is hopping up and down on the bleacher seat next to mine. But she's not the only excited parent, and honestly, she's a hundred times more tame than the family a few rows down who keeps ringing cowbells every time they spot their graduate.

"They haven't brought the teachers out yet, they're still on the communications majors. He'll be walking out soon," I assure her.

Jamie Graham got into town yesterday, making the three-hour drive from Haven alone to see her son graduate college. Apparently, Boone's father was too sour that he never had this chance and didn't want to put aside his own bullshit jealousy to congratulate his kid. But whatever, we were having a better time without him.

Jamie is sweet as sugar, and although I'd seen her around town growing up, we had never been introduced. Not even when Boone and I dated in high school, which was part of the problem back then.

"I'm just so happy to meet you. I know why Boone's been extra

sweet these days on the phone. He has a special someone lighting up his heart."

It's what she'd said when I had gone over to Boone's apartment last night for dinner, and then she'd enveloped me in a hug. I was so shocked, I could barely speak through dinner. But Jamie peppered me with questions, and even gushed about how much she loves my honesty on *Hart & Home*. *"I just can't understand why some of the home buyers want to paint their bathroom green. Or install shag carpeting!"*

And the way Boone adores her ... it's really something. My dad and I are close because we are family and we had no one else for a long time. But the bond Jamie has with her son, it's admirable. She is in touch with his life, follows his accomplishments and discusses baseball as if she could be a coach. She gives just enough criticism and supplements it with encouragement. That is what a mother should be, and I long to hold her attention for as long as she'll give it to me.

"Oh, there he is! BOONE! WOOHOO!" she shouts, pride beaming from every pore.

I look to where she finger points, and there he is. My sexy boyfriend, looking dapper as anything in his cap and gown. I'm proud too, because I know how hard he's worked for this and how difficult it's been to stay in school with the temptation of a million-dollar baseball career hanging just above his head.

He waves up at us, his light hair peeking out from under the cap. It's a little longer than it was just a few months ago, as is his beard, and I find my heart thumping at just how handsome he looks.

The football stadium is packed, which is saying a lot. It seats almost eighty thousand people, and I've been to a few of Cain's games where there weren't nearly as many people as this. Parents, siblings, grandparents, girlfriends, boyfriends ... you name it, there are people out in droves to cheer on their family members as they walk across that stage and receive their degree.

And with this milestone Boone has reached, I also think about how far we've come. Since January, since he came back to Texas. Hate wouldn't even describe what he felt for me then, and heartbreak wouldn't describe what I felt. But slowly, with many months and a lot of time talking, and *not* talking, we've managed to form a relationship. And a pretty great one at that. A supportive, sexy, fun relationship where we lean on each other and don't shy away from commitment.

Except there is one major thing I've been keeping from him, and that pile of papers is currently stuffed in my desk drawer.

"I can't believe he actually made it here." Jamie turns to me, interrupting my thoughts.

Looking down, I see that Boone is now seated, waiting as the rest of the graduates file in and for the commencement speaker to take the stage.

She keeps talking. "I wasn't completely supportive when he said he wanted to get his degree instead of go straight into the league. Selfishly, we could have used the money. But ... I want the best for my child. If he felt he needed to do this, I put my needs and wants aside to let him accomplish his goals. And now, he'll put his all into baseball. And I know you'll be here to support him."

Obviously, Boone never talked about us in high school, or what happened. I'm kind of pissed, but kind of happy that he never mentioned me. That way, this wonderful woman has no ill-feelings toward me, even if I do deserve them for hurting her son.

"I will. I know you don't know me, aside from my TV persona, but I'm loyal. And I'll kill anyone who messes with one of my people."

Jamie chuckles. "I can kind of sense that. And I don't want to speak out of turn, but I understand your hard shell. I won't lie, I've heard about what happened with your mama. Shame, that woman was gifted with a daughter and she took it for granted. Don't ever go thinking that was your fault, though. We are given people to love, and we're supposed to love them. There are some out there who are just too selfish to see that."

I might cry in the middle of this stadium, and this woman who I just met is going to make that happen. I look out to the crowd of graduates below, trying to collect myself.

"Oh, here comes the speaker!" There is a croak in my voice, but I reach over and squeeze Jamie's hand to let her know ... that I just thank her for her words. I hope she understands that.

The commencement guest speaker is a former senator, and while I expect her speech to be boring, I'm surprised by the heartfelt words she imparts on the students sitting here, about to receive their degrees. We clap as she finishes, and we clap and scream even louder when Boone walks across the stage. Others around us point to him and whisper about his baseball career, and Jamie practically beams about the good things being said about her son.

We make our way down together in the swarm of people clambering onto the field to take pictures with their loved one. It takes us a good thirty minutes just to get down the stairs and find Boone among the chaos of bodies.

"Boone!" Jamie runs to him, and even though he has a good foot and sixty pounds on her, she scoops him up in a hug.

"I did it!" He holds his degree up, smiling at me over his mom's shoulder.

I join in, giddy for him, and kiss him full on the mouth while he hugs his mom. The smile that stretches his cheeks is so unlike Boone, and it's making me feel like a schoolgirl watching her crush hug a puppy or something. It's clear he's proud of himself, because he stuck with college even when so many people told him to quit.

His mom lets go, and Boone asks someone nearby to snap a picture of the three of us.

"Have to remember this moment with my two favorite women," he says as he stands in the middle of us, wrapping his tree-trunk arms around both of our shoulders.

I feel like I'm a part of his world, a part of his family. Just like the other night, when I invited him to the Hart's house, and watched him play catch with Ethan. I'd never considered marriage or a having kids as things that I would want in my life. Not that I want them anytime soon, but after my childhood, I didn't think I knew anything about becoming a mother.

It's a long way off, and I'm still not even sure that the traditional life is the one that will happen for me, but ... seeing Boone, at this moment, I want that commitment. It scares me how vividly I can see our lives playing out.

For someone who has tried never to form an attachment to anyone or anything, this man has made me a convert. And I'm surprised to find that my mind doesn't rebel against the idea, but instead keeps imagining further.

W ith the semester over, all of my time is dedicated to the show.

  While my classmates are headed home to lounge around for the summer, or travel, or fetch coffee at summer internships, I'm boots to the dirt day in and day out. I supervise fifteen or sixteen renovations during the summer, a workload that I voluntarily take on to allow James and Ramona to get some much needed down time with the kids.

I'm their wing-woman, their third in command, the work-horse that keeps everyone and everything on schedule.

"Danny, can you please go help Riley bring in and dust off the bookcases? The living and dining room need to be put together by the end of the day, or we won't be on schedule for the reveal on Friday," I ask one of the many assistants who work on the show.

I know that some of the crew think I'm a slave driver, but they just don't understand what goes into keeping this show and business running. And someday soon, I'm going to give it all up to run my own show, be a slave driver for my own crew. The thought both excites and frightens me. I've been waking up in the middle of the night, in the midst of a panic attack, trying to resolve myself with the decision I made.

Even though I still haven't signed the contract.

"Come on, Annabelle, do we have to hang both of those tapestries? Can't we just wait until Jose gets here tomorrow?" Jessie, one of the new design interns whines.

Jessie is on my last nerve. Ramona has been off all week, helping out at the kid's camp, and since Jessie is a year older than me with less of a title, she thinks she can talk to me some sort of way.

And my patience is tissue paper thin. "You know what, Jessie? If you have that attitude, you won't be asked back by Ramona. I'll make sure of it. And not because I have an authority complex, or because I'm a bitch. Because you can call me whatever you want, but I work my ass off. Ramona and James give me so much responsibility because I work until my fingers bleed. Until my eyes won't stay open. Because this is my dream, and if it means standing on a ladder with a laser measuring tape, re-doing the tapestry hang to get it perfect, I'll do it."

She stares at me, mouth hanging open, and someone nearby claps.

I hear the word bitch whispered from Jessie as she turns around and stomps into the house. I just run a hand through my hair and breathe an exhausted sigh. It's been a long day.

Another three hours at the job site and I finally fall into the driver's seat of my car, rubbing my eyes to keep them open. As soon as I pull onto the highway, the Bluetooth in my car starts to ring with a phone call.

I press the button to pick it up. "Hi, Daddy."

"Peaches, how is my girl?" His voice holds a smile, and it makes me smile.

My dad is a good parent, and I am lucky to have grown up

with him. Even if he had the cloud of my mother's desertion hanging over his head for the second half of my childhood, he was still always there. He learned how to cook, did my home-work with me, attended every cheerleading competition, and tried to make our home as normal as possible. I didn't appre-ciate him enough for that.

"I'm good, had a very long day at work. How are you guys?" I turn off at an exit and drive the ramp to another highway.

"Oh, we're good. Honey, I worry about you. You're still a college student, you shouldn't be working forty hours a week." There is a drop of concern in his voice.

I sigh. I haven't told him about the offer from Kutch yet, but I need to talk to someone. And we have daughter-father relative privilege. If I say he can't tell anyone, he won't tell anyone.

"Well, it might ramp up way more than I work now. I got a contract for my own show." I go on to explain the meetings at headquarters, the premise of the show, and how much money I'd be making.

"I don't know, honey ... are you sure you want to do this so early? You haven't even graduated from college yet. Are you sure you don't want a degree? This seems so rushed ... you have all the time in the world. I want you to establish your career on your terms."

"This is on my terms, *Dad*. I don't know why you just can't be happy for me." My tone is cutting, my patience finally snapping from work, and I'm aware I sound like a five-year-old brat.

He sighs. "Anna, I'm so happy and proud of you. You have always done exactly what you wanted, and you've typically been so successful without any help from me. I'm just ... I want you to really think about this before you do it."

When I was younger, and in high school, I entered every beauty pageant I could apply for in the hopes that my mom would see something in the paper or online and come find me.

That she'd be so proud that I won the biggest pageant in the state, and then she'd have to love me or care about me.

In a way, it's the same now. Sure, this deal has its weird stipulations and I am going to fuck over the people who have been so good to me. But ... I always said that when it came to be my time, I was going to be cutthroat. And this was it, I was going to mow down anything in my path that prevents my mother from seeing my image splashed over every magazine and website.

She'll be forced to reach out to me after my show debuts, after it leads the ratings. I will prove to her that I can be just as grand a business woman as she is.

Maybe Ramona and James will understand. They run their own business, they know how it goes.

"Yeah, sure, Dad. All right, I'm almost back to campus, I have to go." I'm so annoyed and don't feel supported whatsoever, and all I want to do is hang up.

"I love you, Peaches," he says, his tone weary.

I hang up without saying I love you, because I'm tired and cranky.

And because, in the back of my head, I know he is right. This isn't the right deal for me, and he is supporting me by being a parent and voicing that.

I should tear up that contract. I should find another way to get my mother's attention.

Finally, someone got through to me. As I drive toward campus, it all clicks. The one parent who has always been there for me has managed to fix the error in judgment I've been sitting on for almost three months. I'm not this person anymore, this selfish, cold person who puts her needs above everyone else. Since Harper and her mother have come into my life, I've been changing for the better. And that has only been furthered with Ramona and James, who are like my second family.

The icing on top has been Boone. He has taught me that

even if I screw up, do my very worst to push someone away ... he'll always be there. That no matter how icy I am to him, we are going to figure out a way to stay together.

Of course I have to say no. Of course I am going to turn them down and go to Ramona and James for advice.

First thing in the morning, I am going to come clean to everyone I've been keeping this from for a while now.

I'm going to come clean.

The sultry notes of *Florida Georgia Line's* "Talk You Out of It" fill Boone's kitchen, and I wipe my hands on the apron I'm wearing.

"I never thought I'd see the day when Annabelle Mills would be in my kitchen, cooking me dinner."

I point the knife I was just cutting tomatoes with at him. "Don't get used to it. I'm far from Suzy Homemaker. But I wanted balsamic chicken pasta and I make it the best, so you get to reap the rewards, too."

Those big hands, toughened from holding a bat and being jammed in a glove every other day, hold my waist, the front of his body coming to snuggle up to the back of mine as I stand at the island, chopping.

"I'd like to reap some other rewards." Teeth sink into my earlobe.

"Just because you put sexy country music on does not mean I'm going to sleep with you." Except that I wiggle my ass a little, in time to the music.

I can already feel the outline of his hardening cock through both of our pants. "It's taken much less, these days."

I swat him in the head and he moves back, letting go of me, laughing. "You're an ass. Now go sit over there before I throw your portion of dinner in the trash. Or better yet, I'll eat all of it."

"Bossy, bossy." He tsks, smiling as he walks over to the living room couch.

The lyrics and melody are the only noises in the apartment as I continue cooking, the silence between us comfortable. We've fallen into a routine, and while I have always thought that would be boring, it's one of the most cherished things in my life at the moment. Knowing that he'll be there to talk to or just to hold at the end of the day, that's the kind of closeness that songs are written about. A closeness I never knew until Boone and I came back together.

"What is this?"

I turn around, and Boone is holding up the top sheet of the contract I'd been mulling over before he got home.

He'd been at the ballpark, playing a game, and I'd had a conference call with a buyer, so I skipped it. I brought the contract with me because of my revelation yesterday.

A thought had clinked off my stubborn brain and rested inside of my skull during that drive. If I'm so embarrassed by this deal, by this show, that I can't even tell my boyfriend about it ... why am I agreeing to it?

"Uh ..." My brain stalls, because I hadn't wanted him to actually see it.

I wish I'd hidden it. There are things in there I don't want him to see. The numbers. The stipulation that I must bare cleavage and say certain sex-laced phrases. The section about the show taking over the time slot currently held by Ramona and James.

The pit in my stomach that has been sitting there since I decided I'd tell Boone, because I was nervous about just telling him, expands until it sinks the organ to my feet. My hands immediately dampen, the back of my neck grows hot, and I realize the instantaneous reaction of shame has taken over my body.

My plan had been to sit him down and talk it through, tell him about the meetings and contract, but not show him the exact details. To tell him how I felt about it, what it meant to me in terms of my mother, and why I'd considered it. I wanted to show him that I'd seen how selfish it was, that I was a day away from turning it down, to telling Kutch no.

This had not been part of my plan. And now I couldn't verbalize a thing.

"You would actually do this to Ramona and James? You would actually do this to yourself? What is this shit, Anna?"

"I can explain—"

"All you care about is being famous, isn't it? About money and the way others view you. You haven't changed one fucking bit. You're still the same exact vain, shallow little girl I knew in high school."

His eyebrows slash in an angry way over his face, and the lips that have given me such pleasure in the past few months are pursed, the lines around them conveying rage. This is the way he looked at me all those years ago on the steps outside of our high school.

A tear slips down my cheek, and I realize I'm crying in front of him. My first instinct is to turn away, to shield myself from him seeing any kind of emotion from me.

But Boone is smarter than that. "You're going to cry now? Are you sorry that I found it, or sorry that you're going to take the offer? Say something, damnit!"

He slams his open palm down on the counter he now stands next to, and my head snaps up.

"I was … was going to decline, I didn't want to—" Words still fail me.

"I was so wrong about you. You'll never change. You're always going to be the self-centered, dramatic mean girl you always were."

I start to cry in earnest now, his words cutting deep. I thought I'd done it, showed them that I could change. Maybe he's right, maybe I am always going to be a horrible bitch. But the hurt comes from deep inside, from never feeling good enough to deserve love. And now it was proven; Boone is looking at me with such hate in his eyes that I know all my worst fears are confirmed.

My entire life, I always felt off when I looked at everyone else. Niceness wasn't my first base instinct, judgment was. I wasn't sure when I became the way I am now, but my first reaction is to be closed off, to be an asshole. My worst fear in life is that someone is going to figure this out, that at my core, I am completely rotten. Because no matter how mean I can be, I still crave the love and attention that everyone else wants. I want someone to work hard enough to see through my hard outer shell.

But here it is, the worst has happened.

The one person who saw through that shell, who decided to love me anyway, has come to the conclusion that I am a terrible person, and there is no longer anything I can do to hide it.

"Get out." He turns away from me as the music changes, the fun-loving Little Big Town track mocking the situation playing out in the apartment.

"Boone, please, I'm so sorry …" I walk to him, reaching out, my brain finally kicking in to survival mode. I have to save myself, I have to save us.

"I said get. Out." The words are spit out as he grits his teeth, his back still turned.

Slowly, with silent sobs wracking my body, I pick up the contract, shove it in my bag, and walk to the door.

I thought my mother leaving was the hardest thing I'd ever have to endure.

Turns out, closing that door behind me was even harder.

37

ANNABELLE

I know I have to go to Ramona, head anything off before she hears about it.

After Boone kicked me out—a thought I can't even think without tearing up—I got into bed for two days and sobbed. Thank God Thea let me sublet her room in her off-campus apartment for the summer, so I at least had some peace and quiet while my heart broke into a million pieces. I'd barely spent any time there at all the past month ... Boone's place had become my place too.

Two days, three boxes of tissues and a *10 Things I Hate About You* bingeathon later, I decide to pull myself out of the breakup hole I've fallen into. My first call is to Kenneth Kutch's office, and I bluntly inform his secretary that I will not be signing the contract and will be staying on in my position on *Hart & Home*. She'd obviously been flustered, and I didn't want to know Kutch's reaction when she told him. Better her than me for the initial news, although I'm sure I'll be hearing something at some point. But I hadn't signed anything, they couldn't come after me. That had been bad business sense on him, sinking money into a college junior that he thought was a lock.

I could admit I was a little scared of what *might* happen though. What if they push me out of *Hart & Home*? Or if Ramona and James fire me. Well ... I would deserve that.

And after that phone call, I put one in to Ramona. She deserves to hear this from me, and I need to come all the way clean. Boone accused me of being a fame whore, of being a selfish mean girl. And I guess I'd been those things by hiding what was going on. I'll take the consequences that come at me for speaking the truth.

Speeding to their farmhouse on the city limits of Austin, I find her in her pantry, re-organizing. There are dozens of cans and boxes around her, kid's snacks and juice boxes and cartons of pasta litter the floor.

When she sees me, her smile goes wide, and she stands up. "Anna! How did you know that I was just contemplating the design of my entire bedroom? Come in, tell me what you think of this canopy bed I just ordered. I might send it back—"

Ramona walks around her house, expecting me to follow like I live here too. And I practically do. I've probably spent more time with her family than I have on my college campus.

I cut her off, stopping in the kitchen as she rambles. "I have to tell you something."

My tone must convey seriousness, because Ramona turns around and there is worry flooded in her green eyes. "What's happened?"

I have to sit on one of the gray metal stools scooted under their white butcher block island. My hands are shaking, because I realize I'm about to disappoint this woman who has always been there for me. Who has been more of a mother to me than my own mother ever was. How could I have been so stupid not to see the wonderful group of people right in front of me? Instead, I've been trying to impress a ghost, a shadow in the wind who never cared to look back for me.

I suck in a breath. "A couple of months ago, Kenneth Kutch approached me about doing my own show. The young, sexy, basically soft-core porno version of *Hart & Home*. There were all of these stipulations in the contract about wearing skimpy clothes and holding tools a certain way. And ... I was going to sign it. I held out, but they had the ball in motion. A photoshoot was done, marketing materials were drawn up, and ..."

I couldn't say the next part. Her face was void of judgment or anger, but I knew she'd be devastated after this one.

My voice comes out in a choked whisper as I cast my eyes down. I can't look at her when I say this. "He wanted me to bump you out of your time slot. They were going to demote the show to the earlier hour."

The breath I'd swallowed was trapped in my lungs, and the shame burning my cheeks made my whole body overheat.

"Sometimes I forget how young you really are because you act so mature. You're even more shrewd than I am at times, and it makes me think you don't need the emotional support that someone your age needs."

That is the first thing that this angel of a woman says to me in response to my betrayal. It makes a sob crack open in my throat, and she clicks her tongue and hugs me. Instead of anger, instead of kicking me out just like Boone did, Ramona holds me as I collect myself.

I shrug, wiping a tear. "I try not to need people. Being clingy or seeking attention has always made people in my life run the other way."

"And those people suck, because a child should never be abandoned or blamed for something they can't control. If a person is not happy, that is their problem. But, you ... you, Annabelle, are a gem. Never forget that."

Sniffing, I finally look at her. "Do you ... hate me?"

Ramona pauses a second, and then folds me into her arms

again. "Oh, honey, I could never hate you. I think you saw the error in your ways, right? Because you wouldn't be here telling me this if you hadn't eventually turned Kutch, that bastard, down?"

I nod, sitting upright once more. "I called yesterday and told his office that I wouldn't be going forward with my own show. I'm sure they'll find a way to kick me off yours. That is ... if you still want me on it."

She gets up, rolling her eyes, and fills the tea kettle with water before putting it on the stove. "Stop with that pity party, of course we want you on the show. You're a part of our family, and the only way you're getting out is in a body bag."

That makes me laugh. "What are you, the renovation mob now?"

"Something like that. But I'm serious, Anna. You're going to be harder on yourself for considering that contract than I could ever be. I'm not upset or angry, you work your ass off and someday, you'll have your own show. Or line. Or whatever it is that you want. You deserve that. But we both know that wasn't the right opportunity for you. And as for Kutch and his minions, I'll handle them. They'll be reminded how much money we bring in for this channel and will have no problem keeping you on because I say so."

Ramona sets two large, white mugs on the counter and plops a green teabag in each. I watch her, taking shaky, relieved breaths.

"I was so nervous to tell you. You ... you and James have done so much for me. I'm sorry I lost sight of that for a second. I'm sorry I let a lot of people down trying to get the attention of one person."

My voice hitches again, thinking about Boone's eyes as he smashed what we had to smithereens.

"Oh, Anna, what else?" Ramona turns around, panic on her face again.

I don't cry, which is probably why she is freaking out every time I show emotion. Turns out, my weakness was a completely split open heart. It apparently has the power to make me a weepy mess.

"Boone found out that I'd been keeping the contract a secret and kicked me out of his apartment. He hasn't spoken to me in almost a week, isn't returning any of my texts or calls. He's done with me." I shrug, my heart literally aching in my chest. "I guess I should have seen it coming, I lied to him. Again. I'm a horrible person."

Ramona clucks at me, her expression annoyed. "Stop saying that crap about one of my favorite women. You're not horrible, you made a mistake. We all make mistakes, it's part of being a human. I'm sure he'll come around in a few days. Just keep on him, keep badgering him, apologizing, anything. Did I not tell you before? Do anything to claim your man. They're lazy, pigheaded and oftentimes don't know their ass from their nose. That's why you have to figure it out for them. He's your one, and you're going to do anything to get him back. I know that because you're Annabelle Mills. And Annabelle Mills gets whatever she wants."

Her pump-up speech, because that's what it was meant to be, fills my broken heart with a little hope. But my spirit is wilted, my pride dashed, and the love I have for him burns like a fresh wound.

It would take a lot for me to pick myself up and go after him, even if chasing him is the only thing I want to do.

F or almost five years, I tried to convince myself that anything outside of baseball and school would distract me. That I had to forgo alcohol and friends and love because it would only bring me down. That it would only destroy me like it had my father.

But since the blowout fight with Annabelle, where I kicked her out, that has proven to be the furthest thing from the truth. I haven't seen her in two weeks, ignored her calls and texts, and since then, everything in my life has gone to shit.

My relationship is obviously in no man's land and isn't coming back anytime soon. I struck out in consecutive games, something I've never done, *ever*. Not even in little league or tee-ball. The other day, I learned that I was turned down for a marketing campaign with a big name sports company. And to top it off, I got my first professional error in our game tonight. I dropped a damn ball because I was squinting into the overhead field lights and lost track of it.

Now, as the road trip bus rumbles along the highway in the dark, I lean my head against the window and sulk.

My heart hurts. Physically hurts. It aches, and my stomach is so sour from the feeling of loneliness invading it that I've had a hard time keeping anything down since Annabelle and I broke up. I miss her, so much that it is even invading the way I play. That has never happened to me before, although I've never been in love with anyone else besides her.

But I couldn't believe her. I'm heartbroken at losing her, but I am also equally as heartbroken by the way she deceived me. When I found that fucking contract, when I read the betrayal she was about to slice Ramona and James open with, I was furious. I wanted to punch a wall but refrained only because my career depends on it.

She had cheated on me, once upon a time, and I'd forgiven her because I thought she was truly sorry, and she'd been a kid back then. But what she was going to do to her bosses? To the people who have mentored her and brought her into their family and home? It was despicable. It was cheating on an entirely different level, maybe even worse than what she had done to me, and she's a grown woman now.

The minute I kicked her out has played over and over in my mind so many times in the last fourteen days. I could barely look at her, but when I did, she looked devastated. I hadn't let her explain, I couldn't bear it. It was the high school steps all over again, with me suffering at the news of her mistake. After she walked out, the apartment felt empty, and her pasta had burned. I threw it in the trash, and went to lie down in bed, but everything smelled of her. The pillows on my bed, the bathroom where she sprayed her perfume, even the couch, where we lay to watch movies.

I hate her. I miss her. I fucking love her. The first round hadn't been hard to end because it was a high school romance, puppy love days. But this? It stings like a cut that keeps getting pried open. Because I've fallen in love with Annabelle, and the heart doesn't forget shit like that quickly.

The bus pulls up to our home stadium, the creak of the door jolting most of us from our post-loss pity parties.

"All right, men, in the locker room. Wash up, get your shit together, and back here tomorrow at eight for practice. This is not a slump, you hear me? Don't let that ole baseball superstition get in your head." Coach walks off the bus, and reluctantly, we follow.

I stay under the hot spray of the shower until my hands and feet are pruned, and then go to my locker to dress and get the hell out of there.

"Boone, can you come into my office?" I turn around to see Coach rapping his knuckles on the doorframe, and then he walks back into his office.

Oh, fuck. This is going to be an ass reaming. I've been playing like shit, I know it, and they pay me to win games. The biggest piece of karma right now would be if I got fucking fired. Because that was just how my month was going.

My feet drag as I walk the short distance to his door, and when I step inside, Coach asks me to close it. I inhale a sharp breath, hoping with all my energy that he's not going to give me the boot.

"Well, kid, it's been a pleasure having you here," he says, his hands folded on his belly as he leans back in his chair, kicking his feet up on the desk in front of him.

My stomach sinks like a fucking stone, and suddenly, a wave of nausea rolls over me. The thing I've been working my entire life for is about to come to an end. I never thought I'd need that fucking college degree, and now I was going to have to use it. I wish I could burn it at this moment.

"But I knew there would be a time where we'd have to let you go, and it looks like it came sooner than I thought. The major league team is calling you up."

A beat goes by. And then another.

"I'm sorry, what?" I must have misheard him.

"They want you on the big squad. You're going to The Show." A tiny smirk crosses his lips.

I go temporarily blind and deaf, not able to use my senses or interpret the world. Is this what happens when all of your dreams come true?

I feel like skipping, or running around in circles, or just acting like a giddy little kid.

My dream, the one I've been working half of my life to achieve, has finally come to fruition. I'm going to the big leagues, I'm going to be at the most advanced level of professional baseball imaginable. I'm going to play on the same fields that my heroes, the legends I watched as a kid, played. I'll be playing with and against some of the biggest names in the game, and some who will go down in history.

"Coach ... I, thank you. Thank you for what you've taught me here and thank you for the support to accomplish bigger goals. I ... don't really know what to say right now."

"You're a good kid, Graham. Dedicated, tough, don't say too much, your ego is in check. You're going to do well up there, and I'm proud to be the one to give you this news." He stands up, offering a hand.

"Thank you, Coach." I shake it, knowing he's dismissing me.

Walking out of his office, I can barely think straight. I should start cleaning out my locker, call my mama, or my agent ... figure out what I need to do in the next few days which are bound to be a whirlwind.

But all I want to do right now is walk out onto the field, smell the grass, take a breath. So I do. My feet take me to the stadium, over to a specific section, and I sit down in a seat.

I don't realize where I chose to sit until I look up at the scoreboard in the outfield. This was the seat that I'd sat next to Annabelle in when I kissed her all those many months ago.

My heart ricochets in my chest, and I know that it is because a small portion of me knows I am missing something to complete this dream. Damn her. Damn that hellcat of a woman, because the only person I want to tell about getting called up is her.

She's become my go-to person. The one I went home to at the end of the day and commiserated or celebrated with. But all that has gone to shit, and it's her fault.

Too bad my heart is taking longer than my head to come to terms with that.

The news of Boone's promotion to the major league baseball team came via an ESPN update, right there on my cell phone screen.

I installed the sports app when we started dating again, so that I could follow any news on him. Boone told me at the time that it was ridiculous, if there was any news I needed to know, he'd tell me before the media got their hands on it. But I thought it was funny, and I hadn't had the heart to delete it off my phone in the almost three weeks since we've been broken up.

I saw the update come through as I hiked up the same trail Boone had once taken me to. The moment I realized what it meant, I looked up to the bright blue sky and mouthed the word *congratulations*. I wouldn't get to tell him that in person, or even in a message since he wasn't returning those ... but maybe the world could deliver it for me.

His dream was coming true, and I ruined any chance of being there with him to see it happen. I wonder briefly, as I come to sit on a rock overlooking the landscape below, if Boone thought about me when he was told the words he has been waiting a lifetime to hear.

Having a week off, in my book, was unheard of. But after my talk with Ramona, and her realization that maybe they'd loaded too much on my plate, she insisted on me taking some time off. To be a young adult, to clear my head, to heal my heart. If she thought I would resist, I must have surprised her. Because I took it, gladly.

I need space, and some time to feel my pain and own what I almost did. On day one of my week off, I sat in bed the entire day reading a book. An actual book, not a textbook, that I became invested in and enjoyed the story throughout. The second day was spent getting a manicure and pedicure, and not having to rush out immediately after to go to class or to a shooting location.

And today I decided that I would let myself unwind in nature. The spot that Boone had taken me to was too off the map and too beautiful to not return to. On a random weekday morning, there is essentially no one here, and I've had quiet time to just ... *be*. Then, the update had come through, and a sparkle of pride shimmered through my chest at Boone living his dream.

There was one more person I had to tell about my news of turning down the show Kutch had pitched me, the one who has always been a silent supporter, whether I asked him to be or not.

"Hey, Dad," I say when he picks up.

"Hey, honey, good to hear from you. Usually your phone calls are few and far between." He chuckles, and that makes me feel guilty. I've spent so much time focusing on the bad parent that I haven't appreciated the good one.

"Yeah ... I probably should call more often." The conversation feels a bit stilted.

But Dad was always a supportive Dad. "No worries, honey, I'm always happy to talk to you."

Might as well just get on with it.

"I decided to say no to the show." My heart feels like it has leapt off a bridge as I say it into the phone.

A sigh comes through on the other side. "I'm really glad you decided to do that. It wasn't the right move, morally or for your career. Can I ask why you turned it down?"

My eyes scan the horizon, the dazzling sun rays making me shield them with my hand. This place is beautiful, serene even ... and I'd admit only to myself that I came here because I wanted to feel closer to Boone again. If I couldn't be with him, then I could go to the spots where we'd once been happy.

"Well, let me first tell you the reason I almost took it." I pause, take a breath. I've never told my dad just how insecure I am over her leaving. "Mom."

"Annabelle—"

"No, let me explain. I know that you have your feelings about her, and I have mine. All I see of how things went down is that she left us. Abandoned us. She fled from her child, the one person she should have loved unconditionally. And she never looked back. For years, I've been trying to get her attention, to be as highly publicized, first in the state of Texas and then the country, as I could be so that she'd take notice. Beauty pageants, good grades, cheer competitions, design projects, the show with Ramona and James ... all of it was to get her to notice. To be proud. And this has nothing to do with you, Dad, if anything, I should have stopped this nonsense and realized I have a great parent right beside me, cheering me on. It's just ... she's my mom. And she left."

He's silent for a beat, but then his voice comes through. "I honestly thought you'd never talk to me about this. At first, I tried to avoid even bringing her up because I was so hurt and scared it would cause more damage to you. But then, we just kind of fell into a routine of never talking about the elephant in the room ... or I guess the elephant who left. You're one tough woman, Annabelle. You've accomplished so much in such a short time, and you don't need her to tell you that. You don't need anyone to tell you that. You should be damn proud of everything you've done and will do. I'm ... I'm a little shocked right now. It's taken you a long time to get here, and I don't want my daughter to push everyone away anymore."

Instead of being sad, I smile, because my limbs, my heart, my soul ... feel light. That heaviness that I've been sitting with for so long feels like it's been lifted from my shoulders. And with it being lifted, I finally feel like I can open up. Who knew, the ice-cold bitch could express her emotions and feelings? I guess pigs really can fly, and maybe hell has just frozen over.

"Thanks, Dad. For listening. I'm finally starting to see that, yes, I don't need anyone else's approval. I've said that I don't care about it for years, but now my internal emotions are maturing enough to realize I actually don't. Maybe I should have major life decision meltdowns more often."

Dad chuckles on the other end. "I think you've taken on about as much as a college student's life can hold ... or maybe a bit more than normal. Slow down for a bit, okay, kiddo?"

I roll my eyes at him calling me kiddo, but I nod like he can see me. "Got it."

"Oh, and tell Boone congratulations from us. We just saw the news about him being called up to the majors."

That one cuts deep. Clearly, Harper hasn't said anything to them about our breakup, and I am thankful that I have a stepsister who is loyal, but also travels and probably has no cell reception where she is right now to even call home.

I do not want to get into that awful subject right now, so I skim over it. "Yeah, sure."

One bombshell at a time is all I can handle at the moment.

40

BOONE

I was right, in that I wasn't prepared for the whirlwind that hit when the news of the major league team calling me up went viral.

The amount of media emails, calls and texts that are coming to my phone is insane. I have been on the phone with my publicist, who was hired this week at the urging of my agent, at least two hours every day.

I've had media training, I knew when to talk and when not to. But this media blitz that has swept in like a crazed tidal wave is a whole other level.

Not to mention the new contracts I had to sign with the team, the trusts and investment decisions I had to make with my financial advisor. And the packing that had to be done to move me an hour away from Austin, to be closer to the major league stadium.

It is all so overwhelming, even though I have a team of professionals practically wiping my ass for me. And all I can think about is getting out onto that field. The massive, stadium-sized bowl of grass was going to be bigger than anything I've ever played on. The rush I get every time I think about how insane those first moments of my first professional game are going to be ... God, I can practically taste it.

Everything is in order for the move. Everything is in order for the next chapter of my life.

Except for one very important, aggravating, beautiful woman who I can't get out of my head, no matter how much I want to.

Annabelle has been leaving me texts and voicemails every day this week. She's persistent, and damned desperate if it's okay to say that. But ... I would be lying if I said she wasn't wearing me down. I have even listened to some of the voice messages this week, her voice making me half-hard. That's what this woman does to me, gets me aroused even when I've broken up with her. She drives me crazy inside even when I don't want to think about her.

She said oh so many things. How she was sorry, how she was proud of me, how she wants to explain the whole story to me. My heart splintered each time she said the word sorry. Anna used the word like it was one of her limbs ... as if giving it to me hurt like hell but she'd do it anyway to prove her point.

I kind of respect her tenacity, that she isn't willing to give up on us. And lately, I've been doubting myself and my actions. How had I given up on us so quickly? I did the exact same thing I'd done back in high school, the exact thing I promised Annabelle I wouldn't do to her again.

I dismissed her from my life without listening to her side whatsoever.

My own emotions are clouding my judgment, because as much as I don't want to see her face-to-face ... I want to see her face-to-face more than anything in the world right now. Maybe even more than I want to play my first game in the majors.

There is only one person I can go to for advice who will shoot it to me straight.

Twenty five minutes later, I walk into a high-tech training

facility on the west end of the city, a place I know a lot of amateur and professional athletes train at in their off-seasons.

"Hey, man."

I stand in the doorway of the training room where Cain is working out. He drops the barbell he's been squat pressing when he sees me in the mirror, standing in back of him.

"Big man on campus! Or should I say off campus now? Either way, you got a big boy contract, my dude." Cain struts over, fist bumping and bro-hugging me when he reaches where I stand.

I smile. "It'll be you soon enough."

"You got that right. And I'm going to sign for more money than you, dude." He takes a long chug of water from the clear Poland Spring gallon by the weight benches. "But you're not here to talk about your contract or your move. You're here to talk about Annabelle."

"How the hell did you know that?" Is it tattooed on my forehead or something?

"Because I've been privy to every girl-code conversation between Harper and Anna for the past three weeks. Believe me, I knew you'd show up on my doorstep at some point. So what's up? You realize you actually love her and can't live without her?"

I eye him suspiciously. "Are you psychic?"

Cain waves a hand at me. "Nah, just have been a dumb-ass myself in the past and know how this goes. All is well, lovey-dovey, hot sex, relationship and then BAM! You or she makes some huge mistake and fall apart, only to realize after that you're meant for one another."

I sit down on one of the benches, my elbows resting on my knees. "Except I'm not sure that this will end in a happily ever after. What she did, man ... it was fucked-up. I don't think she's changed."

"She has, trust me." He looks at me with this weird, intense stare.

"I'm just not sure about that. Annabelle has always been ... distant, cold. Even when we were at our happiest there for a little while, she's a very independent woman. Not that it's a bad thing, but ... I'm leaving. A long distance relationship between the two of us could never work."

Cain sighs and squats down, plopping himself to the ground with his legs outstretched. Then he holds his hands out, gesturing as if to make me see his point coming at me.

"Annabelle got me the second chance that I needed with Harper, and I'd be remiss to not give her the same courtesy. She and I, we're cut from the same cloth. I think I've told you that. We both had our mothers abandon us, so I know what her pain feels like. And I know that doing something desperate to get her mother's attention probably felt rational at the time. But trust me, I've seen a huge change in her the last six months that you all were together. I've seen a huge change in her since she graduated high school. But it's slow ... she's Anna. She's not going to change overnight. And from what I've heard, in the sad phone conversations she's had with Harper, she was going to turn it down, man. You just found her out before she could come clean and admit what she'd been doing. It might sound a little Monday Morning Quarterback, but I believe her. I believe she was going to do the right thing. And I also believe she's crazy about you. So maybe ... maybe you want to hear her out before you leave for the big time and don't get another chance."

I study my hands, the ones that have held bats and baseballs and school pens and laptops ... and Annabelle. Cain is right, I can't leave without seeing her, without hearing her out.

"They always realize, in the end, that they're meant for one another, huh?" I smirk at him.

Cain grins like a cat who caught the canary. "Every damn time."

41

The stairs to the house behind me are old and dilapidated.

I sat on them two hours ago with a sniff at the dirt and a worry that a splinter would go right through my jeans, but I sat anyway.

I'd found it a while ago, this craftsman-style home with a sloping roof and stately front porch. It has promise, needs a lot of work, but with the right eye, it could be beautiful.

The stairs are the things that pulled me back to it, though. There are about twelve leading up to the grand porch and front door ... which are a lot of steps for the front of a home.

But then again, the big moments between Boone and I always happen on stairs. Back in high school, we'd ended on a set. And just a little while ago, my fall down the science building stairs had spurred a reconciliation.

I was hoping that this broken, creaking set would bring me luck today.

After I confessed to Ramona and James, they accepted my apology with open arms. And I asked James to reserve this lot, put it on the back burner and keep it out of the realty listings for a little while longer. I had an idea.

It has taken Cain convincing Boone to come out here and meet with me, and my hands will not stop shaking as I wait for him. When I hear the crunch of his tires on the long gravel driveway to get to the front porch, my heart begins to gallop.

I haven't seen him in three and a half weeks. So when he unfolds his long body from that car, I swear, my mouth starts to water. Damn it, he looks so good. He's let his usual scruff grow out into a little bit of a beard, and it makes him look even more rugged and mysterious than he already is.

"Hi." My hand makes a small wave as he nears me.

We both look uncomfortable. Boone stands at the bottom of the steps, a few feet away from where I sit farther up. "Hey ..."

A beat passes. "Can you sit?"

He obeys but keeps a good foot of distance between us.

"Thank you for agreeing to meet with me. I first want to say that I'm so happy for you. Boone, you did it, you made your dream a reality. I'm really so happy for you."

He tips his head a bit. "Thank you."

Okay, he's not going to make this easy. I deserve that.

I take a deep breath. "I know you might not believe me, but I was going to tell you. That day in fact. I had the contract because I was going to call Kenneth Kutch to turn it down, and then I was going to explain it to you. I was ... it was all about my mother. You have no idea what I have to prove. My mother ... she left us! That show could have given me the platform to show her that the daughter she left behind isn't worthless. She did ..." My voice cracks and I know he can see the tears I've been trying so hard to conceal from him for what seems like a lifetime. "She did so much damage."

I have no idea why I'm getting so emotional out of nowhere, but he's in front of me and it all just comes pouring out. I promised myself that I'd go into this rationally, but I can't hold onto the icy demeanor I've put on for a decade. Not with him, not if I am going to put everything out on the line.

"You don't even realize, Boone. How damaged I was. How damaged I am. When we started talking, dating ... whatever it was that we were to each other, I was already cold. My mom left us, she left me. Her only daughter, her kid. She wanted nothing to do with me, only wanted to exceed in her career. She loved work more than me. And no amount of love from my father or other family members could ever bridge that Grand Canyon-size gap. Each time you picked someone over me, ignored me for sports or friends or just because I really didn't register all that much to you ... it chinked away at what little pieces of my heart still existed. I only had half of that organ when I met you, and with each denial of your feelings for me, more of it crumbled. When you kicked me out a week ago ... I think it just about broke me."

A sob chokes me, and I hear a strangled noise next to me. All at once, Boone is scooping me up into his arms. "I believe you, I believe you."

He rocks me against him, cradling me and kissing my hair. We're apologizing without words, just holding each other and communicating through the healing properties of touch.

"I know that I made a huge mistake. I turned it down. I came clean to Ramona. My dad and I have been talking about how her leaving affected both of us. I won't try to convince you that I'm changed, or that I deserve a second chance, but I just needed you to know all of this."

Boone sits me up, looking straight into my eyes. "I was going to come here and ... honestly, I didn't know what I was going to do. Part of me still doesn't trust you, but part of me is so hopelessly gone over you that I was going to take whatever you said and believe it. I wanted to put up a bigger fight, but I just can't."

He takes my hands, kisses them, and then carefully kisses each cheek where the tears have made paths of sorrow on my flesh. "I understand, probably more than you think I do. I told you why I don't drink, right?"

I sniffle, shrugging. "Yes ..."

Boone takes a deep sigh and looks straight into my eyes. "I've never talked to anyone about this, but I probably should have told you. I should have conveyed just how alike we are. Anna ... half of the things I do in my life, probably more than half, are to spite my father. My senior year, about a month after we broke up, my father got laid off from his job. He had no other real skills, had no college degree, and was too old to be hired anywhere else. So, he turned to alcohol. And has stayed nice and drunk since. It's cost my family nearly everything; my mom has had to work three jobs, I've busted my ass to excel at baseball and in school. His failures have caused my inability to give in to my dream completely. It's why I wouldn't leave school to play professionally. The way my dad has ripped apart my family because of his lack of education, I had to get my degree. I know what it's like to want to prove somebody wrong on such a raw, cellular level. I know how you feel when you feel desperate to act out, to make that person recognize your achievements in any way possible."

I touch his face, feeling his pain as mine while he tells me his story. "I had no idea."

"And you should have. It was all starting to unravel back in high school ... and I won't blame the breakup on that, but I know how closed off I was. I know how I hurt you with my indifference. And ... yes, you fucked-up big time. But I also walked away. *Again*. I should have been a man, stuck through the tough times because that is what I told you I would do. I'm sorry for that."

We've come a long way since that day on the steps, but it is a little bit gratifying to hear him say that.

Boone continues. "I know how you feel, and I want to hold you up and show you the light. The light of how incredibly amazing you are. Annabelle, you are a star on a hit television show, and you're about to be a senior in college. You work with amazing people who can show you so many hidden secrets about the career you want to get into. You are smart, sharp and have a unique eye. You know when to bullshit and when to grit your teeth and smile. You're honest and loyal to a fault. And I know you don't think you are ... but you're kind. You would never turn away a child or a person in need. Outward bubbliness and exaggerated niceness might not be your strong suit, but you are kind. You don't need her approval. The people who love you the most know how incredible you are."

I search his eyes. "I'm not sure I even know how to feel that love."

He puts my hand to his heart. "Feel this. That is love. The love I have for you, because I'm more in love with you than I can ever hope to put into words."

The tears that were already carving paths down my cheeks begin to fall faster. In my life, I have never felt good enough to be loved on such an unconditional level. But by Boone forgiving me for my mistakes, giving me a second chance, and then showing me how his love can help me heal even further ... that ice that's always resided inside my soul melts.

It gives way to emotion that overwhelms me. I bury my face in his shirt and sob. When he tips my chin up, I grin a watery, snotty smile.

"I'm sorry I'm such a mess. That I've always been such a mess."

Those full lips part in a wry smile. "You're so far from a mess, you're intimidating at times."

"I love you, too, by the way." My heart feels lighter as I tell him how I feel, as if it's been waiting to get that cinderblock of emotion off of it for years.

He kisses me until the tears stop, until both of our breathing is ragged and heated. I pull back, snuggling into him, because I just want to hold onto him. It feels like forever since I just held him.

"So, what is this place?" Boone says into my hair.

I pull back. "Well ... I saw it two weeks ago when we were scouting listings for these new clients. And I kind of just ... fell in love with it. I'm not sure why, it needs so much work. I obviously can't afford it. But it ... it kind of reminded me of you."

A grunt of curiosity echoes from his chest, and he stands up and walks down the front porch stairs. That big grizzly of a man, who just admitted he loved me, stands in front of the house I picked for him, hands on his hips, studying it.

Those caramel eyes assess every groove of the roof, the columns on the porch, the front door and shutters. My heart pounds harder than it had when he told me he loves me. Not that I wasn't still internally freaking out about that, but matching people to the home for them is my calling, my passion. And this is the most important pairing I've ever attempted.

"I love it. But ... I'm leaving. Why would I buy a house here?"

I get up and walk down the steps. When I get to Boone, I wrap my arms around him. "Well, at the sake of being nauseously romantic, this is the city that brought us back together. I think it might be nice to have some roots here, even if you're leaving right now. Come on, it's not like you don't have the money. And ... I don't know why, but I just know this is your house."

That smile that hooked me in high school smirks down at me. "You mean our house."

One Week Later

I n the last week, I told Annabelle I love her, bought a house in the town I was moving away from, left said town, received a million-dollar bonus, and am suiting up to play in my first major league baseball game.

To say that I have emotional whiplash would be an understatement.

But as I stand in front of the locker with my name on it in this Texas baseball institution, the stadium I'd now be playing in, I take a moment to pause. Everything in my body is calm, buzzing like an engine about to go full throttle, but at the same time, calm. I am sure of myself, there is no turmoil left.

I accomplished everything I'd set out to. I graduated, and with that degree in my hand, I could let go of all of the emotional baggage where my father was concerned. I don't need his praise, and I don't care that he is downing whiskey at home while Mom sits in the luxury box I reserved for my friends and family tonight. She finally quit two of her jobs, at my convincing. I'll work on making her leave her main source of income, because she doesn't need it anymore. She has more than enough money sitting in her bank account now, I've personally seen to it that it was deposited into a singular account for her and only her. One day, I'll make her see that it is time to leave that asshole ... but for now, I am just happy that I can be the one to take care of *her*, instead of her breaking her back for *me*.

My dream, the reason I wake up in the morning, is finally coming true. In just twenty short minutes, I am going to run out onto that field in front of thousands of fans, and my closest loved ones, to play the game I love. I can't even describe the elation I feel, or the focused adrenaline shooting through my veins. I always imagined that I'd be scatterbrained and hectic at this moment, but it's like I have blinders on. All I can see is exactly how to win this game.

And then there is the greatest thing of all. For a long time, I convinced myself that love was a silly side requirement in life, that I didn't need it to be happy. How fucking wrong I have been? Having Annabelle say those three words to me, and having her here for the past week as we organized and rearranged my life ... I can't imagine doing this without her. After everything we've been through, the breaking up and the fighting and hating and eventually loving ... it all clicked into place. We were meant to go through all of that hell to get to where we are right now.

I bought the house, in the end. Annabelle was right, it is my house. Our house. It's going to be her project to run with, of course, and she said that it would help her miss me less now that we'" be apart a lot.

The idea of that strikes a sharp pain low in my gut. This is the part of love and baseball I have feared ... leaving the woman I want to spend every minute with behind. I heard from other guys in the minor leagues, and always read interviews from the legends, of how difficult it is to miss milestones with their families. That this career means sacrifices in your personal life. I'll be one of those guys now, trying to make time for Annabelle while I play all around the country.

But it won't be like this forever. She'll graduate in a year, and until then we'll figure it out. There is no other option. I am in love with her, and I'll never let anything come between us again.

"Hey, rookie, it's time to go."

Someone claps me on the back and I stand, pulling my brand new hat down low and flexing the brim in.

The rest of my life is about to start.

As they announce my name and number while I jog onto the field, I look up to the box where she sits. There was my woman, wearing my new jersey, her future last name printed across her back. She didn't know it yet, but I was going to make my high school crush my wife someday.

Of course I came to win, but victory and fame don't matter so much anymore.

The biggest prize I ever won is already sitting up in the stands, watching me live my dream.

EPILOGUE
ANNABELLE

One Year Later

"It's about to go live on the website!"

Boone all but squeals. My six foot something, rugged, athletic fiancé just squealed as he refreshes the Internet browser once more.

And yes, you read that right ... fiancé. About a week after he played in his first major league game one year ago, we realized that we were kidding ourselves if we were going to "go slow" with a long distance relationship. We hadn't fought so hard for each other, for love, to just give it up over hectic schedules and constant travel.

We drove, flew, and bus-tripped back and forth for some three hundred and sixty-five odd days to make our relationship work. And then, I finally graduated and could relocate to be with Boone on his days off. During the off-season, we obviously spend much more time together than when he is playing at ball-parks all over the country every other night.

But then a week ago, exactly two months after my college graduation, Boone Graham got down on one knee and asked me to be his lawfully wedded wife, with a hell of a sparkly rock. What? I might be a changed, open, emotional woman, but I am still a materialistic bitch. I love a good diamond ring as much, or more, as the next girl. Don't pretend you don't as well.

I wrap my arms around his waist, peering over his shoulder. "I can't even look, I'm so nervous."

"Babe, it's going to be great. You're going to sell out in like a minute flat. The hype about this has been insane. And I tweeted it earlier today. You know my followers love you." Boone grins at me.

He recently got a Twitter account, which has amassed almost two million followers in a little under a month, and he is obsessed. My fiancé had never been a social media kind of guy, so he was late to the party. It was kind of cute watching him discover how to live tweet *The Bachelor*, which is our guilty pleasure show.

I like to brag that I have twice as many followers as him, and I am not a professional athlete. And then he'll argue that I am a national television star and that isn't fair in the competition for social media fans. We are still annoying each other and having great make-up sex because of it.

As she promised, Ramona fixed everything for me with Kutch and the Flipping Channel executives. I stayed on at *Hart & Home* throughout my college tenure, up until I took a break two months ago. And that had been at Ramona's doing as well. She asked me, at my graduation, what I wanted to do in my career. It took me about a day to realize that I want to take a break from the show to focus on designing my own decor line.

And since the two people who have given me everything already have a line, they gave me a little bit more. Ramona was over the moon that I wanted to release my own collection under her line, and I worked twelve-hour days every day since May to design the twenty pieces that would be featured in my first line.

It helped to distract me when Boone was on the road, and when he was here, he made me coffee and gave me back rubs to help burn the midnight oil.

My mom has never reached out. Not when I got to appear on *Hart & Home* on an arc of my own episodes about a year ago. Not when Boone won the World Series with his team as a rookie. Not when our engagement went viral a week ago. And not now, when my own line on Ramona's decor deal with a giant department store franchise is about to go live.

"There it is!" Boone slaps the counter, and my whole body tingles with excitement and anxiety.

"Oh my God, scroll down." I want to make sure all of the products are there, and that the pictures look amazing. I'll go back later and obsess over them, but for now, I want a quick look through.

My fiancé does as he is told, smart man, and when we get to the bottom of the page, he turns around to give me a kiss on the cheek.

"I'm so proud of you." Those lips go to my neck, and now my body tingles with something else.

It just so happens that Boone has an off day on the exact date of my launch, which I consider fate's good fortune. He is home all day in our apartment about two blocks from the major league stadium. We still own the house on the outskirts of Austin and have made a promise that we will live there during the summers. Eventually, we'll end up back there. I renovated and refurbished the thing within an inch of its former life, and it looks fabulous if I do say so myself. I even built Boone a wood-paneled man cave, all dark oak and forest greens. The biggest compliment he's ever paid me was when he told me that the house reminds him of why he loves Ramona and James' house so much … it reminds him of a family home. That is exactly what I'd been going for.

"Now let's just hope it sells." I hug him hard, hoping that I can bleed some of my anxiety into his thick skin.

"Of course it will. Harper already texted me this morning that she is going to buy one of everything," Boone assures me.

Harper and Cain are stationed in California now. Cain had gotten drafted our senior year to the team in Los Angeles and had become their starting quarterback last September. They got married in a small ceremony in Haven last March after the season ended. I miss our once a month brunches, but we fly back and forth to see each other often, when Boone and Cain play teams nearby enough for us to justify a trip. At least I have Thea an hour and a half away in Austin, where she is working as an interior decorator for a large hotel chain.

Boone closes the laptop, and I whine. "Hey! I want to watch the sales!"

"We're not sitting in front of the computer all day, stressing. Plus, it's my day off. Let's go do something fun."

"Like look at wedding venues?" I grin up at him.

"If that will take your mind off of this, then sure." He shrugs.

I'm a little shocked that he hasn't fought that suggestion. "Really? I didn't think you'd want to do wedding stuff anytime soon."

"I know you've been buying wedding magazines since the day I asked you to marry me. I found them hidden in your bedside table."

It's a white lie not to tell him that those magazines are from five months before he asked me to marry him, but who's counting? I'm a woman who knows what she wants.

"I'm not sure I want to get married here though." I chew my lip, visions of transforming our backyard in Austin into a rustic, floral fairyland dancing in my head.

Boone palms my cheek. "So figure out where you want it to

be, and I'll show up in a tux. All I care about is you coming down that aisle."

They always say you never forget your high school crush.

Well, in my case, that is true. It just took two awful breakups, a long distance relationship, and six years to show me that my high school crush is the man I was meant to marry.

It's a good thing that he feels the same. We both made plenty of mistakes, and I'm not foolish enough to think that there won't be plenty more. But, as I'll be headed for the altar sometime soon, I think the key to marriage is simple.

We love each other more than we annoy each other. We love each other more than our mistakes.

---

ant to read another spicy college romance? Pick up Nerdy Little Secret today!

ALSO BY CARRIE AARONS

Do you want your **FREE** Carrie Aarons eBook?

All you have to do is **sign up for my newsletter**, and you'll immediately receive your free book!

Then, check out all of my books, available in Kindle Unlimited!

Melt

When Stars Burn Out

Ghost in His Eyes

Kissed by Reality

The Prospect Street Series:

Then You Saw Me

The Callahan Family Series:

Warning Track

Stealing Home

Check Swing

Control Artist

Tagging Up

The Rogue Academy Series:

The Second Coming

The Lion Heart

The Mighty Anchor

The Nash Brothers Series:

Fleeting

Forgiven

Flutter

Falter

The Flipped Series:

Blind Landing

Grasping Air

ABOUT THE AUTHOR

Author of romance novels such as Fool Me Twice and Love at First Fight, Carrie Aarons writes books that are just as swoon-worthy as they are sarcastic. A former journalist, she prefers the love stories of her imagination, and the athleisure dress code, much better.

When she isn't writing, Carrie is busy binging reality TV, having a love/hate relationship with cardio, and trying not to burn dinner. She lives in the suburbs of New Jersey with her husband, two children and ninety-pound rescue pup.

Please join her readers group, Carrie's Charmers, to get the latest on new books, exclusive excerpts and fun giveaways.

You can also find Carrie at these places:

Website

Amazon

Facebook

Instagram

TikTok

Goodreads

.

Printed in Great Britain
by Amazon